Zoey
and the
Forest Friends

Written by **E. M. Kelly**

Illustrated by **Tami Boyce**

Zoey and the Forest Friends

Published by Peekaboo Tree Press

ISBN: 978-0-578-77284-4

Cover and interior layout design done by Tamiboyce.com

For
Rorey, Rocky, Zoey, & Penney
May you never lose your childhood spirit,
and may you help us find ours.

Dedicated to
My husband, Tommy, for encouraging me
to keep writing. I love you.

In loving memory of
Chihuahua Lola "Monkey," Boo Boo, Bethany,
and all our beloved pets. We miss you.

"If you want your children to be intelligent, read them fairy tales. If you want them to be more intelligent, read them more fairy tales." – **Albert Einstein**

Zoey
and the
Forest Friends

Written by **E. M. Kelly**

Table of Contents

You are now entering
Matilda's Forest.
Beware of the
Witch and the wolf.

CHAPTER ONE

Zoey Says Goodbye

*C*reeeak!

The sound of the front screen door opening was such a familiar noise to Zoey, but on this morning, it made her heart sink. It used to be a fun sound that meant she was going outside to play. Today it sounded more like a groan. She knew it might be the last time she ever heard that sound.

Zoey stood on the front porch of the cottage and gazed out at the forest, which overlooked Deer Valley. She loved the way the trees opened up around the cottage. This always gave her plenty of room to run. On this peaceful summer morning, the sunlight streamed through the tall trees, and the birds sang their sweet songs as if they were calling her to come closer. She stepped off the front porch and walked towards

1

her favorite tree. It was where Mittens lived. Oh, how she loved his cute, white paws—they made him different from the other gray squirrels.

"Why couldn't it be raining today?" she whispered. As she gazed out at the enchanting forest, she could feel her eyes start to tear up. She knew this would happen. "Not now," she said firmly to herself. Mom and Dad would worry. Then she tucked one of her golden curls behind her ear.

Slam!

This time she jumped at the sound. She knew it was her parents' car trunk closing. Now it was almost time. She could feel her heart start to race.

"Come on, Zoey," called her mother. "We need to get on the road. You know the entire university won't wait for you," she laughed, as she waved for her to come towards their white car.

"That's right, Zoey...you don't want to be late for your orientation, now do you?" asked Zoey's dad. He was already sitting in the driver's seat of their car.

"Alright," sighed Zoey. "Just give me a few minutes to say... to say goodbye." Her parents smiled and nodded. She knew they would understand.

Zoey's light blue eyes scanned the forest, looking for her best friends. She knew they would come to say goodbye, but would she be able to hear them this time? Probably not, but she had to try one last time.

Above her, Zoey could hear the sound of rustling leaves from the lowest tree branch. "Hi, Mittens," Zoey said with a smile. "I hope your allergies don't bother you too much today."

As Mittens dashed down the tree, Zoey could see Matilda, a graceful deer with gold eyes and a heart-shaped nose, slowly limping towards her. Her right, front leg is broken, but she somehow manages to still run right alongside the other deer. I hope her leg is not hurting much today, she thought. Zoey gave Matilda a half-smile. "I knew you'd be here," Zoey said to her. Then she wrapped her arms around Matilda's neck as she had always done.

Matilda stood perfectly still and nuzzled her head against Zoey's cheek. "You know, Matilda...I don't hear you or the other Forest Friends, anymore. I don't know if you've grown quiet, or if I've lost my hearing," Zoey said, as she looked towards the ground. She shrugged her shoulders. "Or, who knows? Maybe, I really have been crazy all these years. Maybe, it was never real, at all."

"No, my dear...you haven't lost your hearing," said Matilda. "You've just lost your childhood spirit. But, we will never stop believing that you'll hear us, again...someday."

Zoey paused and leaned closer to Matilda, but she could hear nothing. At least now she knew for sure. Then, she stood up and gave one last look at the cottage over her shoulder, as she sighed. She was so excited to go to university, but all that changed yesterday. She was busy packing when her parents called her out to the kitchen to tell her the news. "How could you sell the cottage without even asking me!"

she yelled at them, as tears streamed down her face. If she couldn't convince someone in her family to buy the cottage, then today would be the last time she saw her childhood home and her beloved Forest Friends. Her eyes began to tear up again at the thought, but now was not the time to cry. Right now she needed to think of a plan. After all, if there was a problem, there had to be a solution.

She couldn't leave Matilda and the others without a child who would love them and look after them. As she gazed at the cottage, she thought of the only child she knew who would love the Forest Friends just as much as she did. "Rorey!" she said suddenly, as she thought of her cousin. If she could convince her family in Arizona to buy the cottage, she knew Rorey would look after her best friends. A million thoughts raced through her head, as she twirled one of her curls around her finger. She would call them as soon as she got to university.

"I will miss you, my DEER Matilda," Zoey said, as she looked back towards Matilda who had shifted her weight to her strong front leg. "Matilda, I don't know if you can still hear me, but if you can, just know that I'm going to send you someone who will visit you, and love you just as much as I do. It will be a little girl. She has dark curls and wears a ribbon in her hair. I promise she'll look after you all."

Zoey wrapped her arms around Matilda's neck one last time and closed her eyes. The warmth of Matilda, and the sound of her heartbeat, always comforted her. Then, she stood up and waved goodbye to the Forest Friends. She could see them peering out from behind the

4

trees. Mittens held a crumpled up leaf in his hand, which he used to dab the tears from his eyes. Zoro the Turtle slowly approached Zoey.

"Well Zoro, you've come to send me off, have you?" smiled Zoey, as she stooped down to pick up the hand-sized turtle. When Zoey was a small child, she had asked her mother to help her paint the little pink "Z" on the top of her shell, so she would always know which one was Zoro. She gently kissed her shell, as she had done dozens of times before, and softly set her back down on the forest floor.

Zoey turned back towards Matilda and the others, and with a smile as big as she could muster, she blew them all a kiss. "I'll take you with me, right here," she said, pointing towards her heart.

Then, she hopped in the backseat of the white car, buckled her seatbelt, and rolled down the back left window. As the car began to move, she felt her heart slip down towards her feet. She stuck her head out of the window and leaned so far out, that she needed to unbuckle her seatbelt. Then, Zoey looked back at the Forest Friends, one last time.

The car began to glide down the long driveway. Matilda, even with her broken leg, began to gracefully and silently trot alongside the car, down the long driveway and then onto the gravel road. Mittens and the other Forest Friends began to chase behind the car, too.

"Look at them, Zoey," said her mom. "I think your friends are sending you off," she said, as she watched Matilda from the rearview mirror.

"I know," said Zoey, as a single tear rolled down her cheek. "I know."

And, just like that, Zoey was gone. The forest had lost their dear friend.

CHAPTER TWO

The New Family

Matilda knew that the Forest Friends would be lonely now that Zoey was gone, but as the forest's leader, she must keep their spirits high. After all, Zoey did say that she would send them the little girl. But as each day passed, they grew less and less hopeful that she would arrive. But, this particular morning, everything would change.

"Matilda! Maaatillldaaa," shrieked Mittens through his cheeks, which he had stuffed full of acorns. Not only is he easy to spot in the forest because of his white paws, but he is also the loudest creature, and his shrieks had shattered an otherwise peaceful, early summer morning.

"Yip! Yip! Yip!" cried the newborn fox kits, from their near-by den.

"Oh, now look what he's done," griped Penney the Fox. "I just got them settled down after their breakfast!"

As Mittens dashed down a giant oak tree, to the mossy forest floor, Matilda slowly limped towards him. "What is all this yelling about, Mittens?" asked Matilda, in her gentle, motherly voice.

"Hold on, whew...let me catch my breath," said Mittens. "I ran, I mean I flew, I mean, I just had to tell you the...the Ahh...Ahh... ACHOOO!" As Mittens sneezed, the acorns he had tucked neatly into the sides of his cheeks, flew out of his mouth. They hit Zoro's shell, which sent her spinning like a Merry-Go-Round.

"Woah, I think I'm seasick," said Zoro, as her eyes rolled around.

"Slow down, my dear Mittens. I know how your allergies get," said Matilda, with a smile. She pushed a fallen leaf towards him so that he could blow his nose, which he did quite noisily.

"Ahhh! That's better. Thank you," said Mittens.

"Now, what is all this excitement about?" asked Matilda.

"It's the cottage! A new family is moving in," said Mittens. "I saw a little girl with dark curls and a ribbon in her hair. They call her...Ah...Ah...Achoooo!!!" Mittens paused a moment, to compose himself. "They call her, Rorey."

"A little girl...with dark curls? Could it really be her?" gasped Matilda.

She limped up the hill from Deer Valley, to get a view of the cottage. It was the color of buttercups and charmed you with its purplish-red shutters and front door.

As she came up over the hill, it was then that Matilda saw her. It was a little girl with dark curls walking towards the cottage's porch. Her name was Rorey, just as Mittens had said. She was the little girl that all the Forest Friends had so eagerly been waiting for.

Behind her was a tall, dark-haired man with a mustache. He wore a green baseball cap and was whistling as he carried a big, brown box. This was Rorey's grandpa, or as she called him, Papa. Next to the little girl was Rorey's grandma, Nana. She had hair the color of sunshine and blue eyes that sparkled. Walking behind the little girl was a small, and rather chunky, yellow dog wearing a green sweater.

"Come on, Chihuahua Lola," said Rorey, to the little, round dog. "Don't be scared," she said, as she gingerly patted Lola's head.

Mittens could see the little dog shivering from above, as he spied on them from atop the nearest tree. The problem was, he was not a graceful or quiet creature. As he shimmied his way across a long branch, a strong wind blew.

"Ah...Ahh...ACHOOOO!!" As Mittens sneezed, it sent birds flying out of the tree. Blue jays, cardinals, and robins all soared into the sky, as fast as their wings could carry them. All of this commotion caused poor Mittens to lose his balance and take a tumble, landing him right in front of the little girl and her dog.

"Look, Nana, a squirrel," said Rorey, as she pointed towards Mittens.

Chihuahua Lola suddenly stopped shivering. She locked eyes with Mittens and with a loud "Bark!" made two hops towards him.

"Wait, wait, wait!" yelled Mittens, as he let out a quiet laugh. "I...I can do tricks. Yes...tricks. You wouldn't want to hurt me. We can be pals! Yes, yes...pals. Just watch!"

Lola tilted her head to the right. Mittens then scooped up a pile of acorns and started juggling them in the air.

But, the forest's summer wildflowers got the best of poor Mittens' allergies. With a loud "ACHOO!" all the acorns went flying into the air...all but one, which, unfortunately, bopped the top of Lola's head.

Lola glared at Mittens and with a loud, high-pitched "Bark!" took another hop towards him.

"Well, thanks for coming out tonight, folks...you've been a great audience...GOTTA GO!" said Mittens, as he scurried across the yard. All you could see was his gray, bushy tail twitching left and right, as Lola nipped and barked just inches behind him.

"Chihuahua Lola, come back," yelled Rorey, as she cupped her hands around her mouth to make her small, soft voice sound bigger.

"Nana...that squirrel...I think he said something," said Rorey, as she furrowed her eyebrows. "I saw him do a trick, too!"

"Aww that's nice, Ro-Ro," said Nana. "I'm sure you will make lots of new friends here."

Matilda watched the new family, as they unloaded a large truck filled with stacks of big, brown boxes. She was able to get close enough to see the truck's Arizona license plate, which had a cactus in the center.

"She's just as Zoey said she would be," Matilda said quietly to herself, with a smile. Just then Matilda's son, Jax, who she lovingly called, Fireball, trotted up next to her. He was the forest's biggest and strongest buck.

"Could it really be her?" he asked.

"It's time, my little Fireball," said Matilda, with an even bigger smile. Her gold eyes seemed to twinkle in the forest's sunlight.

"Ughhh, Moooom!" whined Fireball. "I'm not little, anymore! And, could you pleaaase stop calling me Fireball in front of the others? It's so embarrassing," he said, as he looked down at the forest floor, and lightly kicked an acorn with his hoof. Matilda gave him her motherly smile, and they both knew the answer to that question.

"Incoming!!!" Just then, Mittens dove into the hole of a tree, in front of Matilda and Fireball. He made it just in time to dodge Lola's final attempt to grab his tail.

"Bark, bark, bark!" Lola yipped, knowing Mittens was trapped inside the tree hole. Her tail whipped, back and forth at her accomplishment.

"You must alert Harry," said Matilda to Fireball. "Tell him there's no time to spare. We will meet in Deer Valley when the sun sets over the cottage."

"I'll do it...I...I can do it," Mittens' shaky voice echoed from inside the tree. His two front paws were sticking just outside of the tree hole. He didn't dare peer out of the tree hole another inch, for fear of Lola's wrath.

"Chihuahua Lola, where are you?" cried out Rorey.

Lola, having been too small to climb up into the tree and look into the hole, soon grew bored and dashed back to the cottage to find Rorey.

"Is she...is she gone?" wheezed Mittens.

"Yes, Mittens, it's alright. You can come out now," said Matilda.

"Whew, that was a close one," said Mittens. "I mean, not that I was scared or anything," he laughed as his eyes darted left and right still looking for the little dog. "That dog is crazy...I mean, what kind of a dog wears a sweater in summer?"

"A dog from Arizona," laughed Fireball.

"You must hurry, Mittens," said Matilda. "You must get word to Harry about the little girl."

"I can...I must!" proclaimed Mittens, as he pounded his little white paws against his gray chest. "I'll show this forest, once and for all, that I should be a respected member of this comm...commu..commun...ACHOOOO!! Community."

CHAPTER THREE

Matilda's Message

In just three leaps, Mittens had climbed the tree to Harry's House, which had a little wooden sign that read "Head Postmaster." The owls had a very big responsibility, for they were the messengers of the forest. They were also the wisest.

"Harry...Harry!" bellowed Mittens. When Harry didn't answer, Mittens threw his head back into the air and used his little, white mitten paws to bang on the arch-shaped wooden tree door. "Harry, hurry! Gather the messengers...we...we don't have much time," said Mittens, with his fluffy gray tail twitching about.

Harry opened the door, yawned, and stretched out his wings. In his sleepy state, he knocked down a neat pile of tree bark pieces that he had stacked on the floor. He stumbled out of the little treehouse, as he rubbed his eyes with his long wings.

"Now, what is all this fuss about, Mittens?" yawned Harry, as he motioned with his wing for Mittens to enter the treehouse.

"It's the cottage...you see Harry..."

"Don't you know we owls are nocturnal?"

"Oh yes, Harry...I know you're not a turtle," laughed Mittens.

"No, no, no...I didn't say *not a turtle*. I said *nocturnal!* That means I sleep during the day."

"Yes, Harry, I know but you see, the thing is..."

"So, how am I supposed to get some shuteye with all this banging about?" asked Harry.

"I know Harry, but if you'll just let me explain..."

"Now, what did I do with those glasses?" asked Harry, as he looked around his little treehouse.

"Your glasses? You left them on your head," said Mittens, as he pointed at them.

"Ah yes. There we are," Harry said, as he slid the glasses down to his big, yellow eyes.

"Now, I see only one of you and not two of you," he said, as he blinked several times while looking at Mittens. "Alright, come inside, and let's get this over with, so I can get some shuteye!"

"Yes, of course, Harry," said Mittens.

"Have you brought the message?" asked Harry.

"Yes, yes," said Mittens.

For a moment, their big, wide eyes just stared at each other.

"Well, are you going to give it to me? Or, should I just sit here until I can guess what it is?" asked Harry, as he crossed his wings over his white and brown speckled chest. He peered at Mittens over his glasses.

"I don't have it," said Mittens.

"Oh, Mittens, really! You know I don't WRITE messages, I merely DELIVER them," said Harry. "I'm not a writer, I'm a messenger!"

"I know, but it's an urgent message from Matilda, and I didn't have time to write it on the tree bark!" proclaimed Mittens.

"What a morning. Well, then let me WRITE down your message on this piece of tree bark, here," huffed Harry. He then grabbed a piece of tree bark from the top of another pile. Then, he picked up a little wooden bowl of crushed, red berries that sat nearby on a little wooden desk. Harry then dipped the tip of his wing into the crushed, red berries.

"Now, say it slowly. I just woke up, for heaven sakes."

"Ok," said Mittens, as he took in a big breath.

"Tell everyone..."

"Yes, yes, tell everyone..." Harry said as he began to scribble the message on the tree bark.

"To meet in Deer Valley..."

"Uh-huh, yes...to meet in Deer Valley..."

"When the sun has set over the cottage."

"Yawn...yes...when the sun has set over the cottage."

"The little girl with dark curls..."

"Yes, yes, the little girl with dark curls..."

"Has just moved in."

"Alright, has just moved in. HAS JUST MOVED IN?" yelled Harry. "Great jumping jackrabbits, why didn't you say so, in the first place?" asked Harry, as he frantically flapped his wings. This caused feathers to fly about the little treehouse. "I must get this to the owls, at once!" Harry slipped the tree bark into a small messenger bag that he wore across his body.

As soon as he was outside of the treehouse, he opened his large wings and flew off into the forest air, before landing on a long branch at the tree next door. This was the home of Ansel, Harry's Head Messenger, like the little wooden sign on his door read.

"Here they go," cheered Mittens with a smile, as he pumped his white paws into the air.

Moments later, the sky was filled with dozens and dozens of owls, carrying their tree bark messages throughout the entire forest. Half of the owls flew the tree bark pieces into every den while the other half dropped them from the sky, landing in empty nests and splashing onto the ponds' lily pads, for all the Forest Friends to see. It didn't take long for word to spread of the little girl's arrival. They say that word spreads faster than a wildfire in the forest.

CHAPTER FOUR

The Little Girl Who Believed

As the sun set over the cottage, every Forest Friend anxiously gathered in Deer Valley. Matilda limped slowly down Deer Trail to stand at her usual place—on top of a large tree stump in the center of Deer Valley. It was the largest tree stump in the entire forest. The shape of the valley was like that of an outdoor auditorium. It helped carry Matilda's voice so that all the Forest Friends could hear the important news.

It was twilight now, and the crickets were lining up for their usual nighttime summer concert. "And a one, and a two," said Frederick the Maestro Cricket. He tapped a tiny twig onto a pebble, then motioned for all of the crickets in the forest to begin their musical entertainment.

"Oh, I hope they play 'Summer Love' this evening," said Nosey Rosey, as she batted her eyelashes. She was a black-and-white tuxedo cat, who was very much in love with Gary the Gray Cat. Nosey Rosey knew everything about everyone in the forest.

"Oh, brother," said Gary, as he curled his long tail over his yellow eyes.

"Quiet down, quiet everyone," yelled Mittens, as he noisily crashed his way through the crowd.

This was the time of day that Matilda's leg hurt more, so she shifted her weight on to her strong front leg for support. The pain from her broken leg was nothing compared to the pain of her broken heart after Zoey left. As she stood on the large tree stump to deliver the forest's most important message, all of the Forest Friends grew quiet. Frederick tapped the tiny twig onto the pebble, to signal to the crickets to lower their musical notes.

"Friends, our time with Zoey was as precious as the morning dew during summer's drought," said Matilda. At the sound of the name Zoey, every Forest Friend lowered their head. "But today is the day we have long waited for. Zoey has kept her promise, and sent us the little girl who will love us and believe in us." The Forest Friends let out a thunderous cheer.

Just then, a cold gust of wind swirled around them, and Matilda looked up to the sky. As the gust of wind died down, Matilda gazed out at the crowd of Forest Friends.

"How do we know for sure she will be the one to save us?" snorted Franklin the Grumpy Possum.

"Yes, how do we know?" chattered the Forest Friends to each other.

"Because she heard Mittens' voice," said Matilda. Each one of the Forest Friends let out a loud gasp.

"Already?" asked Nosey Rosey. "How can she possibly hear one of us, already?"

"Hurry everyone, let's all go and surprise her," yelled Mittens, as he dashed about the crowd, twitching his tail in front of Franklin's face.

"Will you get that tail of yours out of here, Mittens?" griped Franklin.

"Follow me, everyone," yelled Mittens. "Just watch out for Chihuahua Lola."

"Chihuahua, who?" asked Harry.

"Chihuahua Lola," said Mittens. "The little girl's dog."

"Wait, everyone," cried out Matilda. It was then that another strong wind gust came, and the sky turned a murky gray that sent shivers down the spines of the Forest Friends. As they looked up to the sky, the Forest Friends watched, as some of the green leaves on the trees turned brown and floated down to the mossy forest floor.

"Ma...Ma...Matilda," Mittens said with his voice shaking. "I...I think it's starting!"

"He's right," snapped Franklin. "We haven't got time to waste."

"Harry, what do the owls have to report?" asked Matilda.

Harry took out a tree bark piece from his messenger bag. Then, he slid his glasses down from the top of his head. "Now, let's see here…the owls have reported that the entire western forest has lost its leaves," said Harry.

"Oh no!" cried the Forest Friends.

"Matilda, what do we do?" asked Nosey Rosey.

"Winter is surely coming, and without the belief and love of a child, the forest will stay winter, forever," cried Penney. Hearing this had upset her fox kits who began yipping in unison.

"And then, we will all be daaa daaa doomed!" cried Zoro, as she tucked her body back inside of her shivering shell. The Forest Friends started chattering again.

"My dear Forest Friends, we cannot make this little girl believe in us or love us, any more than we could, Zoey," said Matilda. "We must take it slowly, or we could frighten her."

"But, we haven't the time to wait," huffed Franklin. "It took Zoey five years to love us enough that she could hear us!"

"I've got it," declared Mittens, as he raised one paw in the air. "What if we took it slowly, quickly?"

"Oh Mittens, really," huffed Harry. "You're not even making sense!"

"We know our task ahead is great," said Matilda. "Mittens and I will start first thing in the morning. As soon as the sun peeks over the horizon, we'll begin."

CHAPTER FIVE

Rorey Meets the Forest Friends

"Mittens, wake up," said Fireball. Mittens was tucked into a gray ball of fur in his tree nest. "Mittens… psst…Mittens," said Fireball, impatiently, as he knocked against Mittens' tree with his big antlers.

The tree branch with Mittens' nest began to sway side to side, with every knock of Fireball's antlers. Mittens yawned, stretched, and stood up. As he opened his eyes, he realized the whole forest seemed to be swaying about.

"Woah…Woah," yelled Mittens. He lost his balance, sailed out of the nest, and landed right on Fireball's head.

"Come on Mittens, stop fooling around," said Fireball, as he tipped his head down so Mittens would slide off.

"Well, Good Morning to you, too...hmph!" said Mittens.

"Let's go...Mother's waiting," said Fireball. Then he gracefully trotted up the hill from Deer Valley towards the cottage, with Mittens trailing behind.

"Fireball, wait for me!" yelled Mittens. "I haven't even had my breakfast yet!"

Fireball spotted a large acorn and with his back leg, gave it a swift kick, and landed it square in Mittens' mouth.

"Bullseye!" laughed Fireball.

"Very funny!" muffled Mittens, through the acorn.

There at the top of the hill, was Matilda, waiting for them. "Well, my dear Mittens, have we had a rough morning?" asked Matilda, with a gentle smile. Mittens peered into a nearby rain puddle to see his reflection. His bushy tail and gray fur had leaves sticking out every which way, and the large acorn was still sticking out from his mouth.

"Splat!" said Mittens, as he spit out the acorn. "Well, *somebody* decided to toss me out of bed this morning!" griped Mittens, as Fireball snickered.

Creeeak!

The three friends turned their heads at the same time toward the cottage and saw the dark-haired man step out onto the porch. He sat down in a white rocking chair, holding a red coffee mug.

"Ahhh...now, this is the life," said Papa. "Hey, Ro-Ro, come on out here and watch the deer with me."

"Oh no, he's seen us...run!" said Mittens.

"It's alright, Mittens, he's not going to bother us," said Matilda.
Creeeak!

The front screen door opened again. The three friends could see Rorey, as she hopped down from the step onto the porch.

"Papa, look!" said Rorey. "Nana said I can have this!" In her small hand was a red ball.

"Oh, a bouncy ball! I love these!" said Papa. "Here, let me show you." He set his coffee mug on a little wooden table next to the rocking chair and stepped off the porch down onto the sidewalk. "Now, let's see how high it can go!" He bounced the ball over and over, each time sending it into the air, higher and higher.

"Wow, Papa! Let me try!" said Rorey, lifting her hands into the air to reach for the ball. She bounced it over and over, laughing more, the higher it went...until it bounced down the sidewalk and rolled down the hill, towards the Forest Friends.

Mittens began to twitch his tail, as Rorey came within just a few feet of them.

"Not yet," said Matilda to Mittens. "Let her come to you."

"Papa look—the deer!" said Rorey. Papa was back in his rocking chair, reading a book and sipping coffee from the red mug.

"That's nice, Ro-Ro," said Papa. You can play in the yard for a little while if you want. I'll be here on the porch."

Just then, Rorey spotted Mittens in between Matilda and Fireball.

"Hi, I'm Rorey," she said, as she stooped down to get a closer look at Mittens. Mittens stood frozen with his big eyes wide. "Can you do another trick?" asked Rorey.

Mittens, who was still frozen, peered his eyes to the right and spotted an acorn on the forest floor. Then, he slowly tilted his head back and looked straight up. Matilda and Fireball peered down at him, and Matilda nodded her head softly.

So, Mittens picked up the acorn, stuffed it in his right cheek, and held up one of his mitten paws. Then, he stuffed another acorn, and then another, into his cheeks until his mouth was full. He grinned from ear to ear, as Rorey giggled. Being from Arizona, she had never seen a squirrel up close before.

Just then, another strong wind gust came. Uh oh, I'm going to sneeze, thought Mittens. Then, he let out a muffled "ACHOO!" as he spit out every last acorn that was in his mouth onto the forest floor.

Rorey giggled and said, "You're funny...I think I'll call you Sniffles!"

"Bark, Bark, Bark!" Lola came barreling across the yard headed straight for Mittens.

"Oh no, not Chihuahua Lola!" cried Mittens. Then the two of them ran around every square inch of the cottage's front yard.

"Chihuahua Lola, no!" scolded Rorey. "Don't hurt Sniffles!" But, Chihuahua Lola had chased Mittens up a tree and was not going to let him back down. Rorey looked back at Matilda and Fireball. "Hi, deer! I'm Rorey. You don't have to be scared of me."

Matilda carefully took a step forward, limping on her broken leg.

"Your leg!" gasped Rorey. "Oh no, you're hurt," she said, pointing at Matilda's leg.

As Rorey stooped down to take a look at Matilda's leg, another strong gust of wind came, causing more leaves to rain down. Rorey looked up at the sky, watching, as the leaves turned from green to brown as they fell.

Then, just behind Matilda, Rorey saw it—a big, gray wolf that was stepping out of the trees, and walking towards them.

"My, my, my, so this is the famous little girl," said the wolf, as he grinned, showing off his long, yellow teeth. "Really Matilda, I would have thought you would have at least mentioned this to me," said the wolf, as he walked towards Rorey at the bottom of Deer Valley. "But of course, I've been banished from all of your little meetings here."

"Don't take one more step towards her!" shouted Fireball.

"I was only curious," grinned the wolf. Then he turned and looked deep into Rorey's chocolate brown eyes as if he was searching for something. "Little girl, can you hear me?" asked the wolf, as he stared at her with his green, glowing eyes.

But, Rorey just stood there frozen. All she could do was stare at the wolf. It was the first time she had ever seen one.

"Ah hahaha," laughed the wolf, as he tilted his head back into the air. "She can't hear a thing. Oh, the witch will get a kick out of this! I simply can't wait to tell her. You're almost out of time," said the wolf, as he laughed some more.

"Get out of here, Damen!" said Matilda, in a strong voice.

"Why Gimpy Matilda...your leg is looking worse these days," snickered Damen. "Tsk. Tsk. Tsk. It's such a pity. You used to run beautifully, and now you're a cripple."

"Damen, I'm warning you!" huffed Fireball, as he took a step between Damen and Matilda, putting his large antlers in Damen's face.

"My son, his words cannot hurt me," said Matilda to him gently. "Let him call me what he wants. I know my name."

"Rorey, it's time to come in now," yelled Papa, from the cottage's porch. "Come on back up the hill, so I can see you. Nana said that breakfast is ready."

Then, another strong and much colder gust of wind came, which sent leaves swirling around them.

"Well, it seems I must be going," said Damen. "It looks like winter is coming a bit early this year," he said, laughing. "Such a shame...it seems the little girl can't hear us at all," said Damen, with an evil grin. "Oh well, ta-ta for now. And Rorey...I'm sure I will be seeing you again soon," he grinned, as he showed off his long teeth.

Then, he slowly turned his back to them, and sauntered away, silently disappearing into the forest. As he walked away, Rorey saw them...big, red paw prints that slowly faded, one by one, as he walked away.

CHAPTER SIX

New Beginnings

"Papa, Papa!" yelled Rorey, as she dashed back up the hill. "I saw a big dog!"

"You did?" asked Papa. "Where? What did he look like?"

"He was down the big hill! He was big and gray...with sharp teeth!" said Rorey, as she pushed the hair from her eyes. She was still trying to catch her breath after she ran back up the hill to the porch. Papa stepped off the porch and peered around looking for the dog, but he saw nothing but the tall trees.

As they walked into the cottage together, Rorey still couldn't catch her breath. "Nana, I saw a big and scary dog!" said Rorey.

Nana was standing in the kitchen holding a spatula. She was wearing a purple polka dot apron with cherries on it. "You saw, what?" asked Nana, as she spun around.

"She said she saw a big dog, but I couldn't see it," said Papa. "She was just down the hill, and I couldn't see what she was talking about. You know how her imagination gets," he laughed, as he patted her on the head.

"Rorey, don't go to the bottom of that hill, anymore," said Nana, as she gently placed her hand under Rorey's chin. "Make sure to play where you can always see the cottage."

"OK, Nana," said Rorey, as she looked down at the floor. Suddenly, she realized the sweet scent that was dancing its way through the kitchen. "Are we having pancakes?" she asked, with her big, brown eyes.

"We sure are!" said Nana. "You know it sure isn't easy finding things, with all of these boxes to still go through," she said, as she walked rather funnily, through the maze of stacked moving boxes. "But, I found what I needed to make a big stack of pancakes, for all of us. And, since it's such a pretty morning, I thought we could have breakfast on the back deck."

"Yay, then, maybe I'll see Sniffles!" said Rorey, as she dashed towards the back door. She cupped her hands around her eyes, as she leaned against the glass door to look outside for Mittens.

"Sniffles?" asked Nana and Papa at the same time, as they looked at each other.

"She's only been here a day and she's already naming the forest animals," laughed Papa.

As the trio ate breakfast on the back deck, Mittens climbed up the closest tree so he could get a closer look. He scurried to the end of a long tree branch that hung just over the back deck. He had a perfect view of them, as he peered down at the patio table.

"Sigh...it sure is peaceful out here," said Nana. "Nothing like the hustle and bustle of Phoenix."

"Ahhh, and I love to breathe in this clean, forest air," said Papa, as he stretched back in his chair with his arms overhead.

"I'm just so glad, it all worked out," said Nana, as she clasped her hands together. "We can finally relax and enjoy our golden years here."

"Yes, and I know how happy Zoey is that the cottage stayed in the family," said Papa.

Nana and Papa were Zoey's aunt and uncle. After Zoey left for university, she called her aunt and uncle and convinced them to buy the cottage and move from Arizona. She was thrilled when they agreed.

"I know," said Nana. "My sister said that the poor thing was so sad when they told her they were selling the cottage and moving to New York."

"I remember," said Papa, as he took a sip from his coffee mug. "She must have called us a dozen times begging us to buy this place so that she could come back and visit. She was quite persuasive."

Zoey, wanting to keep her promise to Matilda about sending the little girl, had also called Rorey's, parents, Ryann and Ricky.

She told them about a ranch that had gone up for sale just down the road from the cottage. Zoey knew that the Forest Friends would be lonely without her, but Rorey would love them and take care of them. She also secretly hoped that Rorey would be able to hear the Forest Friends the way she used to—they needed someone to talk to.

"Well Zoey should go into sales," laughed Nana. "I never would have dreamed that she would talk Ryann and Ricky into moving here too!"

"That's our clever niece," said Papa between bites of his fluffy, buttery pancakes. "She knew we would never want to live so far away from them."

Nana took a sip from her coffee mug, as she looked around at the forest. "Well, now everyone is happy. We have our dream home for our retirement, and Zoey can visit her childhood home, anytime she wants to. Rorey, are you excited that your Mommy and Daddy will be here, in just a couple of days?" asked Nana. Ryann and Ricky were driving from Phoenix in their moving truck and were expected to arrive at the cottage, soon.

"Yay!!" yelled Rorey. "I miss them," she said, as she stuck out her lower lip into a playful pout.

"I know, but they had to stay back and finish packing up the house, remember? But, they are driving here now," said Nana.

Rorey would soon be reunited with her parents and was looking forward to seeing her new home, soon. It was brown with gray stones that adorned the front. It looked like it was a part of the forest, and overlooked a small pond with a footbridge. And, it was just a short walk from the ranch to the cottage, down a white gravel road. This road led right to the cottage.

"Well, I think it's time to say cheers to our new beginning," said Papa. Then, he raised his red coffee mug in the air and said, "To our new beginning...may we be happy and healthy in this cottage, for years to come."

"And, may I never see another scorpion again," said Nana.

"Cheers to that," laughed Papa, as he clinked his coffee mug with hers.

"I want to cheers, too!" said Rorey. She reached for her cup, which was filled with orange juice, smiled, and proudly said, "Cheers!" as she clinked her cup with theirs.

CHAPTER SEVEN

A New Friend

B efore they could finish their breakfast, a strong wind gust went through the forest, sending a chill through the air. Unfortunately, it caught poor Mittens off guard, and he took a tumble from the tree, landing right on top of the stack of pancakes in the middle of the table.

"Ahhhh!!!" shrieked Nana, as she pushed her chair back faster than a cat can pounce on a mouse.

"Look, it's Sniffles!" said Rorey, as she pointed excitedly. But, before she could blink, Mittens leaped from the patio table and scrambled back up into the tree. In his haste, he managed to tip over a stack of pancakes, knock over the butter dish, and send a pile of napkins sailing into the air.

"Oh, that darn squirrel!" yelled Nana, as she stooped down to pick up the pile of pancakes.

"Looks like we'll be finishing breakfast inside today, Ro-Ro," said Papa, as he picked up a pancake that was still dripping with syrup, off his lap.

Just as they sat down to finish their breakfast inside, at the little round table in the kitchen, they heard *ding-dong!*

"I wonder who that is?" asked Nana, as she put down her fork and looked at Papa.

"Might be a neighbor," he said, as he got up from the table, dabbing his mouth with his napkin. At the door were a tall, yellow-haired woman and a young boy with brown hair and freckles on his cheeks. He had a toy truck in his hand.

"Hi, can I help you?" asked Papa.

"Good Morning," said the woman. "My name is Heather and this is my son, Rocky. We live in the cabin just down the road."

"Well, hello there," said Papa, as he smiled at them. "And, how are you today, young man?" he asked Rocky.

Rocky smiled, looked down to the ground, and said simply, "Good."

"We just wanted to welcome you to the neighborhood," said Heather, as she handed them a basket filled with warm, chocolate chip cookies.

"Well, that's very nice of you," said Papa. "My name is Tim. I just moved here from Arizona, with my wife, Sherry."

"Papa...where are you?!" yelled Rorey, as she came running towards the front door with Nana following.

36

"And, this is my granddaughter, Rorey. She's staying with us for a few days. Her mom and dad are moving here, too. They just bought the ranch down the road."

"Hi, I'm Rorey," she said to Rocky and Heather. "I saw a big dog, today!"

"Oh, really?" asked Heather, with a smile. "Rocky, say hi to Rorey," said Heather.

"Hi," said Rocky, as he smiled, he looked towards the ground again and kicked a small pebble. "This is for you." He handed Rorey a little green truck, which was his favorite.

"Thank you!" said Rorey, excitedly. "Do you want some pancakes?"

"Ya, I love pancakes!" said Rocky, as he smiled up at his mom.

"Well, we shouldn't wear out our welcome," said Heather, as she patted Rocky's head.

"Nonsense!" said Papa. "We're neighbors. Come on in!" They all gathered around the breakfast table, eating the big stack of pancakes and talking about the neighborhood.

Just then, the aroma of the chocolate chip cookies caught Papa's attention. He reached into the basket of warm cookies that Heather had placed on the table. He held a cookie in his hand and showed it to Lola, who was anxiously pawing at his feet, reminding him that she was there to clean up even the tiniest piece. Papa wagged his finger at Lola. Without a word, Lola knew that the answer to her cookie request was a definite, no. So, off she went to her pink dog bed, to sulk.

"We sure were sad when the family who lived here before moved," said Heather, as she patted Rocky's head.

"I miss Zoey," said Rocky.

"Don't worry, you'll get a chance to see her again," said Papa. "She's our niece, and she's going to visit us here sometime when she gets a break from her classes."

"That's wonderful!" said Heather.

"Nana, can I go outside and play with Rocky?" asked Rorey, when they had finished their pancakes.

"Sure, but remember to stay where we can see you," said Nana. The two children scrambled towards the front door and dashed outside with the green toy truck.

"Here, you can have this," said Rorey, as she handed Rocky the red ball she kept in her pocket. The two played together like they had been best friends for years. They took turns bouncing the ball and playing with the truck in the long driveway. But their favorite game soon became hide and seek, as they ran around a large, oak tree, they named *The Peekaboo Tree*. They laughed and squealed, as they chased each other.

Rocky, having been taller and a whole year older than Rorey, instantly became protective of her. "Don't go too far, Rorey!" he would yell if she strayed too far from the cottage. "Careful! Careful, Rorey," he would say if she ran too fast. Then, he would chase after her and take her by the hand, when she would trip and fall.

After playing several games together outside, Rorey spotted Mittens, who was watching them from a nearby tree.

"Hey, there's Sniffles!" pointed Rorey. "He can do tricks!"

Creeeak!

The front screen door opened, and Heather came outside.

"Rocky, tell Rorey goodbye. We don't want to be late for church," said Heather.

"Aww Mom, can't I stay here and play more?" pleaded Rocky, who was out of breath from running.

"Don't worry, you can come back and play with Rorey, again," laughed Heather.

"Bye, Rocky," said Rorey, as she smiled and waved.

Nana and Papa walked outside to wave goodbye to their new neighbors.

"Nana, I like it here," said Rorey, as she hugged Nana's leg.

"Haha, well good," said Nana. "Because I think we're all going to be here, for a very long time."

CHAPTER EIGHT

Saving Rorey

The next morning, as the sun rose over the cottage, Mittens and Fireball snuck over to the cottage. They stood silently, just outside the downstairs' bedroom window. Mittens hopped on to Fireball's head, so he could peer inside, too. They could see Rorey still asleep, with Lola curled up into a ball next to her.

"Rorey, it's time to wake up," said Nana, as she entered the bedroom. "I have a surprise for you."

"A surprise?" asked Rorey, as she sat up in her bed and sleepily brushed her dark curls from her eyes. "What is it, Nana?"

"Your Mommy and Daddy are almost here," said Nana.

Now, she was awake! Rorey kicked the covers off her bed and scrambled to the window. She peered out the curtain and saw her parents' car driving down the long driveway to the cottage. As she dashed outside, she saw her mom open the car door.

"Mommy!" yelled Rorey, as she ran across the mossy forest floor in her bare feet and pink nightgown.

"There's my little Ro-Ro," said her mom, Ryann, as she stooped down to pick her up. "Here, these are for you," said Ryann, as she handed her a bouquet of buttercup flowers. Rorey loved to sniff flowers, ever since she was a baby. When she was a good girl, her mom would often buy her flowers. While other children would get toys, she would get flowers.

She smiled brightly, sniffed the flowers, tilted her head back, and said "Ahhhh!" It always made her mom laugh.

"Mommy, I met a squirrel...his name is Sniffles!" said Rorey, as she brushed her wild, brown curls away from her eyes. Just then, the driver door opened and her dad, Ricky, stepped out of the car. "Daddy!" yelled Rorey, as she dashed towards him.

"Hi, my little princess," said Ricky, as he bent down to hug her.

"Bark, Bark, Bark!" Rorey's eyes got wide, as she pointed to the backseat of the car.

"Boo Boo and Bethany!" she squealed, with excitement.

Boo Boo and Bethany were her family's two basset hounds. Boo Boo had a brown star on his head, with one eye brown and the other blue. Bethany had brown freckles that spotted her white nose.

"Alright you two, it's time to get out," said Ricky. He opened the back door, as the two whining basset hounds flopped out.

They ran right for Rorey, covering her in a pile of wet-nosed kisses. The more she giggled, the more their tails wagged.

"Well, you're just in time for breakfast," said Nana. "Let's get you inside, so you can get settled in. You must be exhausted, and I'm sure you'll want to just relax here before you have to start unpacking."

As the family walked to the cottage's purplish-red front door, Matilda stood in the yard watching. She shifted her weight onto her strong front leg.

"Mother, is your leg hurting you badly?" asked Fireball. Even though she never spoke of her leg, he would notice when it would bother her.

"It's not too bad, my dear," said Matilda, as she nuzzled her head against his. He would only worry if he knew the pain it caused her.

"Mommy, I want to show you Sniffles!" said Rorey, as she bounced up and down and followed them into the cottage.

Matilda smiled, as she watched Rorey go inside. "This reminds me of when Zoey first moved in," said Matilda to Fireball.

"Yes...we haven't had that kind of childhood spirit at the cottage, for a long time," laughed Fireball. "Do you think she can hear us, yet?"

"It's hard to say," said Matilda. "She heard Mittens the first day, but she doesn't seem to hear the rest of us, yet. But, it's a very good start."

Just then, Matilda and Fireball heard the flapping of wings. It was Harry who landed next to them.

"Matilda," said Harry, as he cleared his throat. "The owls have been surveying the forest." He reached into his messenger bag and pulled out a tree bark piece. He set it down on the ground for them to read. The message read:

"The eastern forest's leaves have turned brown and fallen."

Then, Harry took out another tree bark piece from his messenger bag. "Matilda, this is from Ansel. He is my most trusted Head Messenger." He set the tree bark on the ground next to the other one.

The message read:

"The wolf has told the forest's witch about Rorey's arrival. She will arrive at the cottage before the sun sets."

"That filthy, good for nothing wolf!" yelled Fireball, as he angrily stomped his hoof on the forest floor.

Matilda looked up to the sky and closed her eyes for a moment. It was when she did her best thinking, and the Forest Friends knew not to disturb her. As the wind began to swirl around them, Matilda remembered the day the forest's witch tried to steal Zoey's heart and childhood spirit when she was five years old. Matilda knew that without a childhood spirit, the witch's icy heart would stop beating and she would lose her terrible powers.

As ugly and vile as she was on the inside, the witch was beautiful and enchanting on the outside. She wore a white dress that glimmered in the sunlight, and ruby red flowers in her hair.

Everyone was drawn to her...everyone that is except for children. They would get goosebumps on their arms and could feel the hair on the backs of their necks stand up when she came near them.

Years ago, when Zoey was just a little girl, the witch had visited the cottage a few times, to earn the trust of Zoey and her parents.

"Zoey, would you like to pick wildflowers tomorrow with me?" asked the evil witch.

"That's a great idea!" said Zoey.

"OK, then why don't you meet me just beyond those trees tomorrow morning," said the witch, as she patted Zoey on her head. Matilda could hear the witch talking to Zoey, as she hid close to them behind a nearby oak tree. Matilda knew that Zoey couldn't be left alone with the witch. She would always stay close by when she saw the witch come near the cottage.

The next morning, as Zoey ran away from the cottage, a big, gray wolf stepped out of the forest.

"Damen, stop!" cried out Matilda, as the wolf snuck up behind Zoey. Matilda knew the only chance at saving Zoey was to see if she could hear her voice. She cried out: "Zoey, run!"

Suddenly Zoey stopped running and turned to see where the voice came from. She saw no one standing there except for Matilda. Then she saw the wolf.

As the wolf approached Zoey, Matilda put herself between them. "Zoey, run!" Matilda yelled again. This time, Zoey did as Matilda said and ran back towards the cottage.

"Grrrr...get out of my way, Matilda!" growled the wolf. But Matilda stood there like a statue.

"Mother, no!" cried out Fireball, as he leaped out from the forest. As Matilda turned to look at her son, the wolf grabbed Matilda's right, front leg with his big, yellow teeth. He bit down hard, as she kicked and squirmed to get away from his mighty jaws. Fireball raced towards them, and with one swift kick from his back legs, he knocked Damen to the ground.

Even though this terrible encounter with the wolf happened many years ago, Matilda could still remember it as clearly as if it happened yesterday. Matilda opened her eyes and looked down at her broken leg.

"Harry, you must get the word out to the Forest Friends...we must stop the witch from visiting the cottage," said Matilda.

"But...but Matilda, how?" stammered Harry.

"We will need every Forest Friend to help us," said Matilda. "Tell everyone to meet in Deer Valley, before the sun has set over the cottage. We will stop her there."

"Yes, Matilda," said Harry. Harry took out his little wooden bowl with the crushed, red berries, from his messenger bag. Dipping the tip of his wing into the bowl, he began to write down the message onto a tree bark piece. Then, he flapped his wings and soared into the sky.

"Mother, how can we stop her?" asked Fireball.

"My son, we all need to work together," said Matilda. "We must save Rorey, just as we saved Zoey."

CHAPTER NINE

Hearing Mittens

While the Forest Friends began to get word of the witch's arrival, Rorey played in the cottage's front yard, unaware of what was heading towards her. As her mom and dad relaxed on the front porch, after their long journey from Arizona, Rorey decided to wander down the driveway to look for Mittens.

"Sniffles...oh, Sniffles," called out Rorey. "Where are you?"

Matilda, who was just down the hill, could hear Rorey's voice. "It's Rorey!" said Matilda, as her eyes lit up. "We must hurry and get Mittens! We need to find out for sure if she can hear him," she said to Fireball.

Fireball trotted towards Mittens' tree. He was curled up in his nest, taking a midday nap. "Mittens, wake up!" called Fireball. But, Mittens only rolled over and pulled a pile of leaves over his head.

"He asked for it," said Fireball, as he knocked his large antlers against the tree. This shook the tree enough to knock Mittens out of his cozy nest, and he landed squarely on Fireball's head.

"I think you're starting to enjoy this, Fireball!" huffed Mittens.

"Sniffles...oh, Sniffles" called Rorey.

"Mittens, she's looking for you!" said Fireball.

"Sniffles, who is Sniffles?" asked Mittens, as he yawned.

"That's you, and if you don't hurry up, I will toss you from your bed every morning, until eternity," yelled Fireball, as he tipped his head down so Mittens would slide off.

"You just cost yourself a Christmas card!" said Mittens, as he raised his little fist in front of Fireball's face.

"Sniffles, there you are!" cried out Rorey. Just then, Mittens dashed towards her. "I brought you a snack," she said. Then, she shoved a whole peanut butter cracker into his mouth, causing Mittens to look like he had the forest's biggest grin.

"Hahaha!" laughed Fireball.

"Sniffles, can you say something, again?" asked Rorey. Just then, Matilda slowly trotted towards them.

"Mittens, say something," said Matilda, hastily.

"I can't!" muffled Mittens, through the peanut butter cracker that was still wedged into his mouth. He pounded on his white chest with his mitten paws. "Cough, hack!"

"Hehehe," giggled Rorey.

"I'll help you, Mittens," said Fireball, as he grinned. Fireball stooped down and blew in Mittens' face.

"Ahhh...ahhh...ACHOO!" sneezed Mittens.

"Hehehe," giggled Rorey, holding her hand over her mouth. Mittens had sneezed peanut butter crackers all over Fireball's face.

"Serves you right!" said Mittens.

"You CAN talk!" said Rorey. Mittens looked up at her with big, wide eyes.

"Yes, of course, I can!" said Mittens.

"Rorey, don't be afraid," said Matilda. Rorey turned and looked at Matilda.

"Bark, bark, bark!"

"Oh no, not Chihuahua Lola, again!" said Mittens. Lola chased after Mittens, growling, and yipping, as Mittens scurried up the nearest tree.

"Rorey, it's time to come in now," called Ryann, from the front porch. "Nana said that lunch is almost ready."

"OK, Mommy," said Rorey. "Bye, deer!" she said, as she waved to them. Then, she ran down the long driveway towards the cottage.

"This is so frustrating," said Fireball. "Now, we won't know if she can hear the rest of us or not before the witch gets here."

"I think she heard me," said Matilda.

"What...how do you know?" asked Fireball.

"Because she turned her head when I spoke to her, not when I first trotted up. She didn't even know I was there until I spoke to her. And, now we know for sure that she can hear Mittens."

"Well, you can't know for sure," griped Franklin, who was resting under a nearby bush. "And, even if she can hear us, who's to say she will even trust us? And now, we might be too late before that witch and her mutt come here tonight."

"It's not too late," said Fireball. "We will stop them...tonight."

CHAPTER TEN

The Witch and the Wolf

As the sun began to slowly dip towards the horizon, all of the Forest Friends had gathered in Deer Valley. Whenever the witch would come near the cottage, the crickets would not play their musical notes. Tonight, the forest was so quiet, you'd never suspect a single creature called it home. While waiting for Matilda to speak, the Forest Friends began to whisper to each other.

"Oh Gary, I'm such a scaredy-cat," said Nosey Rosey, as she curled her tail around Gary's nose. "I overheard the owls at their meeting, saying that the forest has now lost more of its leaves!"

"No wonder they call you Nosey Rosey!" said Gary. "You're always snooping into people's private conversations!"

"Shhhh, be quiet, everyone!" yelled Mittens, from the front of the crowd. "Matilda is on her way." Matilda slowly walked to the tree stump to stand at her usual place in the center of Deer Valley.

"My friends, tonight we must work together, to stop the witch and the wolf from getting to the cottage. If we fail, she will charm Rorey and her family, and trick them into being her friend," said Matilda.

"And, we all know what can happen next," said Fireball.

Matilda nodded her head in agreement. "We're all going to stand united and not let her pass," said Matilda. "If we work together, we can stop her."

"But, Matilda, she has magical powers!" cried Penney, over her yipping fox kits.

"Yes, and Damen will hurt us!" cried Nosey Rosey.

"Harry, we will need your messengers to swoop down from the sky," said Matilda. "And, all of the foxes, surround the witch in a circle when you see her, so she can't break free. Mittens, I'll need you to lead the squirrels to distract them."

"But, who is going to take care of me?" said a deep voice, from behind them. Matilda turned around and saw a pair of glowing, green eyes staring out of the forest. "Is it you, Matilda?" smiled Damen, as he stepped out of the shade and into the sunlight.

"I'll handle you, Damen," huffed Fireball, in a deep voice. As Damen and Fireball locked eyes, that's when they saw her...the forest's witch, Esmerelda. She glided gracefully towards them, with her white dress shimmering in the twilight. Her feet never touched the forest floor...she merely floated above it.

"I hope I'm not interrupting your little meeting," said the witch, in a soft voice that could still cut through your bones. She stared at Matilda with her icy blue eyes. "Why Matilda, you're not looking well these days," she said, with a crooked smile. "I do think you've let yourself go, my DEER sister. Sigh...if only Mommy and Daddy could see you now. They've been worried sick about you...ever since you and that son of yours disappeared, so many moons ago."

The witch glided towards them until she stopped at Damen's side. She scratched behind his left ear and gave him a playful pat on the head, as he panted. His evil grin grew wider.

"How very sad they would be, to know the truth," said Matilda. "That I was betrayed by my sister."

"Hmm...I suppose you're right, Matilda. I mean, I never could impress them as much as you...you were perfect at everything," said the witch. "But, now that you've been gone so long, I'm afraid that I am their one and only daughter."

"How could you?" said Matilda. "How could you turn your sister and nephew into animals?"

"Matilda, really!" laughed the witch. "Don't be so dramatic. I didn't turn you into a beast. I turned you into a graceful deer—you always did have such grace."

"Used to have such grace," smiled Damen, as he glared at Matilda's broken leg. The witch reached down to scratch Damen behind his ear, again.

"In fact, you should be thanking me. I gave you another chance at life. I gave you a voice and made all of the other little animals able to talk, so you'd have company."

"Thank you? You're a monster!" yelled out Fireball.

"Is that any way to speak to your aunt?" snapped the witch. "I mean, I could have separated you two, forever. But out of the goodness of my heart, I kept a mother and son together, forever," she said, as she clasped her icy, white hands together.

"What did we ever do to you, Esmerelda?" asked Matilda.

"Ha! As if you don't know!" she laughed. "Matilda, when you were around, I was invisible. You excelled in everything— school, dancing, everything! Everyone loved you more. And, when your equally perfect son, Jax, came along...no one even knew I was there!" The witch glared at Matilda and Fireball, and her icy blue eyes flashed red. Then, she softened her face and smiled.

"But, let's forget all this unpleasantness, shall we?" laughed the witch. "After all, I'm here to welcome our new neighbors. I heard the little girl simply loves flowers!"

The witch pulled out a slender, glowing white wand from her shimmering dress. With a couple of twirls of the wand, she made a rainbow-colored bouquet of wildflowers appear.

"You leave her alone!" Matilda said, with a raised voice. Damen and the witch looked at each other for a moment and burst into laughter.

"Oh, Matilda...did you really think you could stop me?" asked the witch.

"I can," said Fireball, as he took a step towards her.

Just then, a light flickered over the hill towards the cottage.

"Look at that...I believe they've just turned on their porch light for me," said the witch, as she twirled in a circle.

Creeeak!

Everyone looked up the hill towards the cottage, as they heard the front screen door open.

"Quickly Damen, we must hurry!" said the witch, as she raised her dress off the ground, so she could dash up the hill.

"Stop them!" cried out Matilda.

Just then, the owls swooped down from the trees, dropping tree bark, sticks, and rocks on top of them. The foxes began to circle the witch and Damen, closing in on them. Damen bared his teeth and let out a low growl. He sunk low to the ground, ready to pounce at the slightest thing that moved. But before he could move, Fireball stuck his large antlers in his face. While the Forest Friends nipped and pulled at the witch's dress, Mittens clawed his way up to her shoulder.

"Get off of me, you vile creature!" shouted the witch, as she snatched him from her dress and flung him to the ground. She pointed her wand at Mittens, but Harry swooped down to carry Mittens out of the way, just in time.

During the chaos, the witch snuck through the foxes' barrier and disappeared up the hill, towards the cottage. Now, they were too late to stop her, for if they got too close, the humans might see them.

"Matilda!" cried Mittens. "What do we do now?" he asked, as he picked leaves and twigs out of his mangled fur. "Esmerelda is going to the cottage to meet Rorey and her family!"

"We do the only thing we can do," said Matilda. "We must get word to Zoey. She will help us protect Rorey."

"But, Matilda, Zoey can't hear us, anymore!" cried out Zoro, from inside her shell.

"Yes, she's lost her childhood spirit," cried out Nosey Rosey.

"Then, we will help her get it back," said Matilda. "We must remind Zoey, of who she is."

CHAPTER ELEVEN

Finding Zoey

The Forest Friends fled up the hill towards the cottage, being careful to hide behind trees and bushes, to keep a close eye on Esmerelda. Damen took off into the forest, leaving nothing but those big, red paw prints behind.

Nana and Papa were on the porch, sitting in their rocking chairs. Esmerelda walked gracefully down the driveway towards the porch.

"Why hello there, neighbors," said the witch, in her friendliest voice, as she stepped up onto the porch. "I'm Esmerelda, and I wanted to welcome you to the neighborhood." She handed Nana the bouquet of wildflowers.

"Hello," said Nana. "We weren't expecting company, at this hour," she said.

"Oh, yes, of course," laughed the witch. You see, I live in a cottage myself, just through the woods. I saw your porch light on through the trees, and realized I must have new neighbors."

"It's nice to meet you, Esmerelda," said Papa.

"My, that is a lovely dress," said Nana.

"Thank you! I'm going to a dinner party, but I wanted to say a quick hello, while I was on my way through," she said.

"And, thank you for the flowers," said Nana. "Our grand-daughter, Rorey, loves flowers. And, these are her favorite kind."

"You don't say!" said the witch, as she smiled and clapped her hands together. "I would love to meet her sometime. I just ADORE children."

"She's just getting ready for bed," said Nana. "Her mother and father just moved here too, from Arizona, and they are staying with us for a few days until they get their ranch down the road a bit more settled."

"How wonderful!" said the witch. "I simply can't wait to meet the rest of your family."

"Perhaps, we could have you over for dinner, soon," said Papa.

"Yes, we'd love to get to know more of our neighbors," said Nana. "I imagine it will take a couple of days for us to get settled in, so how does Friday evening sound?"

Esmerelda smiled. "Friday would be perfect," she said. "I hope you and your granddaughter enjoy the flowers," she said, with a smile.

The Forest Friends, who were spying on them, let out a quiet gasp.

"Pssst, Matilda! Friday is only two days from now!" whispered Mittens.

"Yes, how on earth are we going to get Zoey here, in just two days?" griped Franklin.

"Harry, you and the owls are our only hope," said Matilda. "You must fly to Zoey's university and get word to her about Esmerelda."

"Bbb...bbb...but Matilda," stammered Harry, as he nervously pushed his glasses back on to his beak. "What if she can't hear me?"

"You must write down the message on the tree bark," said Matilda.

"I'm going, too," cried out Mittens.

"Oh Mittens, you will never be able to get there in time!" huffed Nosey Rosey.

"There's no time for this," yelled out Fireball. "We are wasting precious time. Harry, take the message with you and fly as fast as you can. I will take Mittens with me. I can run fast."

"You will?" asked Mittens, with his big eyes. Then, he ran over to Fireball and gave him a big kiss right on the tip of his nose.

"Ewww, what are you doing?" asked Fireball. "You're not starting out well on this trip, Mittens!"

"Be safe, all of you," said Matilda. "We will keep a watch on Damen and Esmerelda, in the meantime."

With that, Harry took out the crushed, red berries, dipped the tip of his wing in them, and wrote down a message for Zoey.

The witch and the wolf are coming for Rorey, on Friday. Please help us, Zoey.

Love, the Forest Friends

He slipped the tree bark message into his messenger bag, along with his glasses and a little brochure about Zoey's university, which had a map on the back. Mittens had stolen it from the family's trash can and kept it, in case the Forest Friends ever needed to find Zoey. The Forest Friends didn't know that Mittens had slept with it in his nest, every night. It always made him feel closer to her. He reluctantly went and retrieved the brochure from his nest and gave it to Harry. And with that, Harry took two flaps of his large wings and soared into the now, completely dark forest sky, unaware that they were being watched, as Damen was peering at the Forest Friends through the tall trees that surrounded the cottage.

"So, they think they can stop us, do they?" asked Damen. "Well, let's just see what happens when Harry loses that message."

And with that, Damen took off running into the forest, following Harry as he floated above, blissfully unaware that he was being followed by the wolf. Fireball tipped his head to the ground so that Mittens could climb on top.

"On Dasher, On Dancer, On Comet..." yelled Mittens, as he raised his mitten paw into the air, while his other paw held on to Fireball's antler.

"Mittens, what are you doing up there?" barked Fireball.

"I'm pretending I'm Santa Clause," said Mittens. "I guess that makes you Rudolph."

"You'd better hold on tight, Santa Clause," huffed Fireball, as he took off running into the forest.

"Woooaaah!!" yelled Mittens, as he wrapped his paws around Fireball's antlers.

"Well, I guess there is nothing left to do now, but go to sleep," yawned Penney. Her fox kits always made her so tired by the end of the day. "Don't worry, Matilda. If Damen and the witch come back, we won't let them get away this time."

Matilda smiled at her and looked around at the Forest Friends. She knew it wouldn't be easy to get word to Zoey, in just two days. But, she also knew she had to leave the Forest Friends with hope.

"Friends, let's all wish a safe journey for Harry, Mittens, and Fireball. We must trust that they will get word to Zoey, in time," she said. Then, a gust of wind swirled its way through the forest. This one was stronger and colder than ever before. The Forest Friends all huddled together and shivered.

"Hahahahaha," laughed Esmerelda, as she glided off into the forest. "Oh, at this rate, Matilda, you will be destined to be a deer, for the rest of your life! You can't possibly win the love and belief of this child, in just two days! And, I'm afraid, my DEER sister, that's all the time you have left." Then, she turned and looked at the Forest Friends with her icy blue eyes.

"I will see to that, and turn this wretched forest into an eternal winter!"

As the witch's glowing, white dress disappeared deeper and deeper into the forest, a pile of dead, brown leaves rained down from the treetops behind her. Then, her dress slowly turned a dark, deep red, before she disappeared into the night.

"Matilda, I'm scared," said Nosey Rosey.

"There's nothing to be afraid of, dear Rosey," said Matilda. "This time it will be Zoey who saves us."

CHAPTER TWELVE

Rocky's Warning

D^{*ing-dong!*}

The sound of the doorbell rang through the cottage.

"Now, who could it be at this hour of the morning?" asked Nana, as she walked towards the front door. She yawned, as she tied the belt around her morning robe, which was covered in pink flowers.

Rocky was standing at the door with a big grin. He wore a dark t-shirt with a green truck on it and his favorite blue shorts that had stripes going down the sides. He would tell Rorey, and anyone who would listen, that he would only wear shorts with stripes because they could make him run faster and jump higher.

"Hi," said Rocky. "My mom said I could play with Rorey today if that was ok with you."

Nana smiled at him. "Well, of course, it's ok!" she said. "In fact, I'm glad you're here so early."

"You are?" asked Rocky, as he batted his eyes at her.

"Yes...you see I have a serious problem," said Nana. "It seems I made too many pancakes, and I don't have enough people to eat them. And, I don't want to throw them away either."

Rocky's eyes lit up. "I know what to do! I could help you eat them!" he said.

"Well, I guess that would make some sense," said Nana, as she pretended to think it over. Then, she smiled down at Rocky and motioned him towards the kitchen table. She pulled out one of the chairs and gave the seat a couple of taps.

He sat down in the chair and said, "Oh boy! I sure do looove pancakes!"

Just then, they heard the sound of pitter-pattering feet, upstairs. It was Rorey. She could smell the pancakes, so down the stairs, she went, almost two at a time. She was pulling her mom's arm behind her.

"Rorey, I just woke up!" said Ryann, as she yawned.

"Mommy, I want to find Sniffles, today!" proclaimed Rorey. As she came around the corner, she saw Rocky and smiled from ear to ear. "Hi, Rocky! Are you going to play with me, today?"

"Yup," said Rocky, as he stuffed a big bite of pancake into his mouth.

"Yay!" yelled Rorey. "Then, can you help me find Sniffles? I want to show my Mommy how he does tricks."

"Why does she keep talking about that awful squirrel?" asked Nana, as she shook her head.

"I don't know...where's the coffee?" asked Ryann, as she shuffled in her slippers on her way to the kitchen.

Just then, Rorey saw the bouquet of wildflowers on the kitchen table.

"Flowers! Can I smell them, Nana?" she asked.

"Why sure! In fact, these are for you," said Nana. "Esmerelda, our new neighbor, brought them over."

"Where does she live?" asked Ryann, as she sat down at the breakfast table with a piping hot cup of coffee. The steam rolled off the top, as she blew on it to cool it down.

"She lives in the scary part of the forest," said Rocky, through a mouthful of pancakes. "I don't like her."

Nana raised her eyebrow. "Really? Why not?"

Rocky shrugged his shoulders and stayed quiet for a moment. All you could hear was the swooshing of air as he swung his feet back and forth in the chair. Ryann peered over at him as she blew on her coffee. "Her house looks scary. And, she has a big dog that looks like a wolf. He looks mean," said Rocky.

"Oh my," said Nana. "Well, then I do think it's a good idea to not go near her cottage. You never know if a dog like that will bite."

Creeeak!

The front screen door opened, and Papa walked in whistling. "Good Morning, sleepyheads. You all are missing the wildlife out there. It's another beautiful day."

Nana yawned. "I didn't get much sleep last night. I could hear the wind howling."

"Oh, you'll get used to the sounds of the forest," said Papa, as he kissed her on the forehead. He sat down in the only empty chair around the breakfast table. "Well, Good Morning to you, Rocky, my boy," said Papa, as he patted him on the head. "I see you've joined us for pancakes, again...smart lad."

"Yup, I sure am," said Rocky, as he shoved the last big bite of pancake into his mouth. "My Daddy likes pancakes, too." It seemed that Rocky's Daddy, also, would exercise and go to work. These were the tidbits of family life that he liked to share with others at any time, for no particular reason, and oftentimes, in no particular order.

"Well, then you should invite him over, next time," said Papa.

"OK," said Rocky, as he smiled. Then, he looked across the table at Rorey who was peering at him over a stack of pancakes.

"Rorey, do you want to go outside and play, now?" he asked.

"Ya!" said Rorey, as she pushed her chair back from the table.

"Not yet, Ro-Ro," said Ryann. "Not until you finish at least some of your breakfast."

"Shhh...do you hear that?" asked Nana, as she waved her hands, motioning them all to stop talking.

"Hear what?" asked Ryann and Papa, at the same time.

"I...I thought I heard a scratching noise," said Nana.

Papa began to move his index finger around in a circle next to his head.

"Cuckoo, cuckoo," he said.

"Cuckoo, cuckoo," said Rorey and Rocky in unison, as they laughed.

"Stop it, I'm not crazy," said Nana, as she lightly slapped Papa's arm. "Shhh...there it is again."

Then, they all heard it and looked up. Above the kitchen table in the ceiling was a small, round skylight. As they all looked up, they saw Nosey Rosey, the black-and-white tuxedo cat, peering down at them.

"Oh, my goodness, what is a cat doing on our roof?" said Nana, as she flung the kitchen towel from over her shoulder down onto the breakfast table.

"Look, Mommy, it's a cat!" yelled Rorey, as she pointed up.

And with that, Rorey and Rocky scurried out the front door, looking for their new, furry friend. Nosey Rosey hopped from the roof onto a nearby tree limb and slid down the tree trunk. Matilda had enlisted her help to try and draw Rorey out of the cottage, so she could try and speak to her again. Her plan worked like a charm.

"Don't go down the hill, you two," yelled out Nana, to them. "Sigh...I'm beginning to feel a little *too* close to nature, in this house."

"Mom, don't you think it was odd about what Rocky said?" asked Ryann.

"What did Rocky say?" asked Papa.

"Well, he said he didn't like Esmerelda," said Ryann. "But, he wouldn't say why...other than her house was scary, and she had a dog that looked mean."

Papa laughed. "Well, you know how a little boy's imagination can run wild," said Papa.

"I don't know," said Ryann. "I didn't meet Esmerelda, but I got the feeling there is something about her that Rocky was trying to warn us of."

"I think you need to drink more coffee," said Nana, with a smile. "Esmerelda was very sweet, and even brought us flowers. You'll see when you meet her. She's coming over, Friday evening. We're having a barbeque."

Ryann shrugged her shoulders. "I guess, we'll find out then," she said.

CHAPTER THIRTEEN

The Lost Message

"Fireball, will you at least try and slow down a bit," said Mittens, as he bobbed up and down on Fireball's head. Fireball was running and leaping at full speed, through the forest.

"I'm sorry I can't give you first-class service on this flight, Mittens," said Fireball. "We've got to get to Zoey."

He weaved in and out of trees, hopped over rocks and roots, and leaped over creeks as easily as if he had been taking a relaxing stroll. But then, he suddenly skidded to a complete stop. Mittens, who was not ready for this, went sailing into the air, like a gray furball.

"Now, what's the big idea?" yelled Mittens, as he picked leaves out of his bushy fur.

"Paw prints," said Fireball. "Red paw prints."

Mittens' eyes became big and wide, as his mouth dropped. "Damen must have just been here!" said Mittens.

"He must have heard us and is following Harry!" said Fireball. "Quick, climb back on, and hang on tight. We've got to follow the tracks before they fade away!"

Mittens scurried back over to Fireball, climbed up his head, and grasped his antlers, as tightly as he could.

Just up ahead and across a large creek, they saw him: Damen. He was following Harry's every move, from down below. He had been silently trotting after him all night, watching as Harry glided through the moonlit forest. Now, the morning light was peeking over the horizon.

"Whew, I need to take a rest," said Harry, as he landed onto a tree branch. He slipped the messenger bag with the message for Zoey, onto the end of a tree limb. What he didn't know, was that Damen was hiding behind a nearby tree, just a few feet below him. Then, Harry pulled out his glasses and the small brochure about Zoey's university, with the map on it.

"Alright, now let's see where we are, here," said Harry, as he looked over the map. "It's just now starting to get light out. If I rest here for a few moments, I can still make it before the sun sets tonight. This will leave us one day to return with Zoey to the cottage. This should give us just enough time to stop Esmerelda."

Just then, a strong wind gust cut its way through the forest, like an icy knife. The wind caught Harry off guard, and it caused the messenger bag to slide off the end of the tree branch and down to the forest floor, below.

"Oh, fiddlesticks!" said Harry, as he hopped up and glided down to retrieve the messenger bag. But, he was too late.

Damen was standing over the messenger bag, grinning at Harry. "Looking for this?" he said, as he put one big, red paw print onto the bag.

"D…D…Damen…you give that back," said Harry, as his voice shook.

Damen tilted his head back towards the sky and let out a loud laugh.

"Give it back to him," said a loud, low voice. Damen whirled around in surprise. He saw Fireball standing there, with Mittens on his head.

"You fool," said Damen. "Do you not remember what I did to your mother? You can't imagine the amount of pain I will begin to inflict upon you." He snapped his teeth at Fireball.

While Damen was distracted, Harry quickly hopped on top of the messenger bag, latched it with his claws, and took flight. Damen whirled around, hearing the sound of flapping wings, and caught the tip of the messenger bag with his teeth. This caused the little wooden bowl with crushed, red berries and the tree bark with Zoey's message, to fall out.

"Go!" yelled Fireball, as Harry sailed into the night sky. Luckily, he still had the map.

Damen spun back around to glare at Fireball. Then, he picked up the piece of tree bark with the message for Zoey and held it between his mighty jaws. With two quick bites, he had chopped it up into little pieces. Then, he spit them out of his mouth. His face softened, and he smiled at Fireball.

"Well, I guess my job here is done," said Damen. "I mean, it's not like Zoey will be able to hear you two or Harry. And, without that tree bark message, well, I'm afraid you will be too late."

"She will hear us!" yelled Mittens, who was quivering on top of Fireball's antlers.

"Whatever you say," said Damen, as he rolled his eyes. "Well, I'm sure Esmerelda will want to hear how I stopped you from giving the message to Zoey. She will probably give me a big reward. She knows deer meat is my absolute favorite." And with that, he sauntered past Fireball and Mittens, back towards the witch's cottage, in the darkest part of the forest.

"Don't worry about him, Fireball," said Mittens, as he patted him on the head. "Zoey will hear us...I know she will."

Fireball lowered his head. He knew that Zoey had lost her childhood spirit before she had left for university. Slowly over time, she heard them less and less, until one day, she couldn't hear them at all. And, without her childhood spirit, she wouldn't be able to hear any of them. How would they warn her about Esmerelda? How would they save Rorey?

Fireball started walking and raised his head, looking up at the now fading moon. "I hope you're right Mittens," he said. "I hope you're right."

CHAPTER FOURTEEN

The Witch's Trick

"Prrr…prrr…" purred Nosey Rosey, as Rorey gently pet her head.
"Aww, you're a nice kitty," said Rorey. Nosey Rosey was curled up in Rorey's lap, blissfully forgetting for a moment, how Gary had dismissed her love, yet again, during last night's dinner.

Matilda slowly approached Rorey, as Rocky played in the driveway with his favorite toy truck.

"Hi deer," said Rorey, as she looked up at Matilda. "Aww, your poor leg," said Rorey, as she furrowed her eyebrows. Matilda slowly limped towards her and lowered her head.

"Aww, you're so sweet," said Rorey. She slowly reached out her hand and gently pet Matilda on the head. "You're so soft."

Meanwhile, the Forest Friends were anxiously watching this scene, from behind the nearest trees and bushes. Penney was trying desperately to keep her fox kits quiet, so she could hear them from her nearby den. Franklin and Zoro were watching nearby, too.

"I wonder if Harry has made it to Zoey, yet?" asked Zoro.

"Hmmph, well, he'd better hurry because the wind is getting stronger and colder, each day," griped Franklin. "And, I for one, cannot live in a forest that has winter for every season! I'm just not built for it!"

"Well, neither am I!" said Zoro, and then, tucked her head back inside her shell.

"You're a pretty deer," said Rorey, to Matilda. "How did you hurt your leg?" she asked. Matilda looked at her with her loving, gold eyes.

But, before she could utter a word, a voice from beyond the trees said: "You shouldn't pet wild animals, little one."

Rorey and Matilda both turned their heads around and saw her. It was Esmerelda. She glided towards them, with the sunlight dancing off of her snow-white dress.

"I heard you like flowers," she said to Rorey. "Here," she said, as she plucked a ruby red rose from her hair and handed it to Rorey.

Rorey's eyes grew big, and she reached out her hand to take the flower. But, as she stared into Esmerelda's icy blue eyes, she suddenly froze.

"My Mommy says I shouldn't talk to strangers," said Rorey, as she looked down to the ground and placed her hand at her side.

Esmerelda's fake smile melted away with surprise. "Ohhh, yes, of course," she laughed, as she tried to regain her composure. "But, you see, I'm not a stranger. I'm your new neighbor, Esmerelda. I met your Nana and Papa, just yesterday. Did you like the wildflowers?" she asked.

Rorey looked up at her and smiled. "Yes, thank you," she said. Her mother had always taught her to thank someone when they gave her a gift. Matilda, who was still standing next to Rorey, nuzzled her head against Rorey's hand to get her attention away from the witch.

"Aww, you're such a nice deer," giggled Rorey, as she pet Matilda's head. "She likes it when I pet her."

"Well dear, I really don't think your Mommy would want you petting a wild...creature," said Esmerelda.

"In fact, I have a better idea!" she said, with her devilish half-smile. "Your Nana and Papa were kind enough to invite me over for dinner, tomorrow night. Would you like to help me pick wildflowers for them? I think they would be ever so surprised!"

Rorey jumped up quickly and said, "Yes!"

"Oh, that's marvelous!" said Esmerelda. "Let's hurry now before the sun starts to set. We don't want to lose daylight."

But, Rorey just stood there silently. It was clear that something was bothering her. She twirled a brown curl around her finger.

"Hurry now dear, we don't have much time," said Esmerelda, waving her on with her right hand.

"I can't go now," said Rorey. "I have to ask my Mommy first."

"Ask me, what?" asked a voice from behind them. It was Ryann, who had heard them from the nearby open window of the cottage. As Ryann stepped out onto the porch, Nosey Rosey pounced in front of the witch. She arched her back and let out a terrifying hiss. Ryann raised her eyebrow at the cat.

"What is with this...cat?" asked the witch, as she tried to hide her rage with a laugh.

"It seems she doesn't like you very much," said Ryann.

"Hmm...yes...so it seems," said Esmerelda.

"So, what's this about taking my daughter with you, somewhere?" asked Ryann, as she folded her arms.

"Oh...oh, you see, I was going to take her just over there into the forest, to pick some wildflowers. I've been invited over for dinner tomorrow, and I wanted to bring a gift," said Esmerelda.

Creeeak went the front screen door of the cottage. It was Nana, who carried out a tray of lemonade and sugar cookies.

"Hello, Esmerelda," said Nana. "What brings you by?"

"Oh, I just happened to be in the neighborhood," laughed Esmerelda.

"I see you've met my daughter," said Nana.

"Well...well, not properly," said Esmerelda. "I live in the cottage, just down the way in the forest. I'm Esmerelda," she said.

"Yes, I gathered that much," said Ryann, without returning Esmerelda's smile. "I would appreciate it if you asked me first, before offering to take my daughter, somewhere," said Ryann sternly.

"Ryann," whispered Nana, as she nudged her back with her elbow, still holding the tray of lemonade and cookies.

"Yes, of course," said Esmerelda. "I do apologize for the...misunderstanding." Nana gave Ryann a look. It was the kind of look a mother gives their child, right before they get a good tongue lashing, in private.

"But, you see, I was only trying to get her away from that wild animal," said Esmerelda. She always thought of a lie quickly, when she needed to charm or trick someone. "They are dirty creatures with ticks and diseases," she said, as she glared at Matilda.

"Rorey, you shouldn't pet wild animals like that," said Nana. "Go inside and wash your hands."

"Sorry, Nana," said Rorey, as she began to silently wipe away the tears with the back of her hand, as they streamed down her sweet face. She did not like to displease anyone.

"Oh, for heaven sakes," said Nana, as she shook her head. "She's so sensitive, we can hardly scold her at all, without her getting upset."

"I feel so dreadful about all of this," said Esmerelda. "It's all my fault. I shouldn't have said anything."

"Oh, don't be silly," said Nana. "I'm thankful you were here to stop her. There is this awful squirrel that she's been calling Sniffles, and I really don't want her adopting him as our next pet."

"Yes, it's probably best if she didn't go near the forest animals, anymore," said Esmerelda, as she glared at Matilda.

"Rorey has always loved animals," snapped Ryann. "Well, it was nice to meet you Esmerelda, and I guess we will see you tomorrow, for dinner." Then, she whirled around and walked into the house briskly, to find Rorey.

"You'll have to forgive my daughter," said Nana, as she smiled at Esmerelda. "She gets a little protective of Rorey."

"Why, of course, she does," said Esmerelda. "Please tell them both I'm sorry for the mishap. I look forward to seeing you all, tomorrow evening."

As Esmerelda turned to walk away, she caught sight of Matilda and the other Forest Friends. Then she smiled and said, "See you all, tomorrow."

CHAPTER FIFTEEN

A Surprising Reunion

"Whew...huff...almost there!" said Harry, as he glided down onto a long tree branch, high off the ground. Down below, he could see tall, grand buildings. They were covered in matching red bricks, with crisp white trim that decorated the windows and peaked roofs.

"Look at all of these people," said Harry to himself, as he peered down at the students. Some were sitting in a grassy area having picnic lunches, while others were bustling along little concrete walkways, carrying bulky backpacks.

"Now, I wonder where I will find Zoey," thought Harry. The map did not tell Harry which dormitory Zoey was to be staying in.

"Hmmm...if I stay here long enough, I'm bound to see her walk by, at some point," thought Harry. "Yes, yes, that's what I'll do," he said to himself. "If she doesn't walk past me by the time the sun is directly overhead, I will set out towards the dormitories."

Harry stayed in the tree and waited. He waited, and he waited. He saw many girls with yellow hair, but alas...none of them were Zoey. She had perfect, golden ringlets that went every which way as she walked or ran, so he knew he would spot her easily.

After several hours of waiting patiently in the tree, he spotted a young girl with her signature golden curls. "It's Zoey," said Harry, as he felt a lump well up in his throat. She had a pink backpack on and was talking and laughing with another young girl with brown hair.

"What do I do now?" said Harry, with a panic. "I can't just fly down there and hope that she recognizes me!"

So, he decided to follow the girls, instead. He let them pass by and silently glided in the sky, above their heads. They were blissfully unaware and trying to decide which class was harder...math, or earth science.

"I think earth science is harder," said the girl with the brown hair. "Plus, it's just boring! I mean, who wants to study and play with rocks, for the rest of their lives?" she asked.

"Mr. Hammond, that's who," laughed Zoey, along with her.

"So, what are you majoring in, anyway?" asked the brown-haired girl.

"Well, I haven't decided, yet," said Zoey. "But, I know I want to work with animals, someday," she said, with a soft sigh. Then, the girls made a sharp left, as they walked along the paved paths of the campus. "Well, I need to go back to my room and study for a test tomorrow."

"Ok, I'll see you tomorrow," said the brown-haired girl, as she stopped at the first dormitory.

Zoey kept walking, while Harry continued to glide above. Then, she turned left again and went into the third dormitory. The sign on the door read "Butterfield Hall." Along the way, Harry noticed other students passing by and saying hello to her. It seemed that everyone on the campus was already friends with their dear, Zoey. As she entered the building, Harry saw her open a door that led to a staircase.

"But, which floor is hers?" thought Harry, as he rested on the ground for a moment.

"Hey, cool. Look at this owl," said a boy with dark brown hair. He was leaning up against the dormitory Zoey had just walked into. This spooked Harry, and he flew up into a nearby tree and perched on its tallest branch.

By this time, the sun was beginning to set. "We've only got one day left," said Harry. "I've simply got to make contact with her, tonight."

So, he flew up to each window looking in with his large, yellow eyes, to see if he could find Zoey. Many of the blinds and curtains were open. He saw two boys playing guitars and singing, which sounded more like screeching. Then, he flew to the next window and saw a girl painting her toenails bubblegum pink. She was talking on the phone: "I don't know, but I think he's going to ask me out," he could hear her muffled voice say.

Then, she looked up from painting her toenails and spilled the pink liquid all over her white bedspread. "Ahhhh!" she screamed, having been frightened by Harry. He quickly flew off, having been just as startled as she was.

He flew around and around the building, looking into the windows, to try and spot Zoey. By the time he had reached the third floor, he saw her through the window that was on the back corner of the building. She was sitting at a little white desk, typing on a laptop.

Now that he knew which room was hers, he needed to think of a plan. So, he perched himself on top of the nearest tree outside of her window. He looked through his messenger bag, hoping to find a shred of a crushed berry, so he could write Zoey a message. But, the wolf had taken everything, except for his map.

"Well, I will just have to get her attention," said Harry to himself. And with that, he flew back over to Zoey's window. There was just enough of a ledge so he could perch his rather large body, momentarily. Then, with the tip of his beak, he began to lightly tap on the window.

Zoey turned around and was startled to see him. "Oh, it's an owl," she said, as she stood up and walked to the window. She unlocked it and opened it with all her might, for the window was rather difficult to open.

"What are you doing here, Mr. Owl?" asked Zoey, with a smile, as she leaned on the windowsill.

"Z...Zoey...it's me. It's Harry," said Harry, with his voice shaking.

But, Zoey only stared at him. "Well, it's silly of you to be perched on this little window ledge. Now off you go, back to your tree," she said, as she shooed him away.

Harry flew away from the window and looked at her in disbelief. His heart was broken, for she didn't hear his voice, nor even recognize him.

He flew back to the tree and dabbed the water from his eyes with the tip of his wings. By now it was twilight, and the sun was cascading its last bit of light across the sky.

"This light...it is just the amount of hope, I have left. And, it's fading fast," said Harry, as he began to cry.

"Psssttt...Harry...hey, Harry," said a small voice from down below.

Harry looked down and saw Mittens, hiding underneath a nearby shrub that was tucked up against Zoey's dormitory.

"Mittens?" asked Harry, through his sobs.

"Harry, it's ok. We made it," said Mittens. "Fireball is hiding behind the building, so he's not spotted so easily."

Mittens looked left and right, and once he deemed it was safe to come out, he climbed up the tree to where Harry was perched. In his clumsiness and usual loudness, he managed to send twigs and leaves cascading down to the ground. This was much to the dismay of the little bluebirds, which were happily resting in their nests.

"What happened?" asked Mittens, when he reached the branch where Harry was perched.

"She...she didn't hear my voice," said Harry. "She's gone...she's really gone."

"Now Harry, we can't give up, so quickly. We only just got here!" said Mittens. "You show me where her window is, so I can get her attention."

Harry finished dabbing the tears from his eyes with his wing-tip. "Alright, I think I can get you up there," he said.

He grasped the back of Mittens' neck with his claws and flew him up to Zoey's window ledge. Then, he flew back to the tree and waited, as if he had been hunting for a mouse. Down below, he saw Fireball's large antlers peering around the corner of the building.

"Zoey...oh, Zoey!" yelled Mittens, from the window's ledge. But, she was busily typing away at her desk and paid him no attention.

So, he decided to pound his paws against her window, as loudly as he could. She quickly spun around in her chair, startled to see a squirrel banging against her window. They were, after all, three stories above the ground.

"First an owl, now a squirrel!" she said, as she walked towards the window. Again, she unlocked it and used her might to force the window back open.

"How did you get up here?" asked Zoey.

"Well, I just flew in from out of town," joked Mittens. "It's good to see you, kid."

But, Zoey merely stared at him in disbelief.

"Zoey, are you coming with us?" asked a voice from Zoey's room. "We're all going down to the dining hall," said a young girl, who was Zoey's age and had yellow hair that just brushed her shoulders. "What are you doing?" asked the girl.

"There's a squirrel on the window," said Zoey.

"Really? That's weird," laughed the girl.

"Yes, and I'm worried he won't be able to get himself back down," said Zoey.

"You and animals," said the girl, as she rolled her eyes. "You're like a magnet for them or something."

"You go ahead, and I'll meet you in a few minutes," said Zoey.

"Ok, suit yourself," said the girl, as she shrugged and then, closed the door behind her.

Zoey peered out the window, hoping that the poor squirrel would be able to safely climb back down. But, that didn't seem to be the case.

"Zoey, can you really not hear me?" asked Mittens. "It's me… Mittens! Your buddy. Your pal! We used to make mud pies and collect acorns together, remember?" Mittens stared at her with his lower lip now starting to quiver.

But, Zoey just stared at him, unable to hear anything at all.

"I guess I'm just another squirrel to you, now," said Mittens, as he lowered his head. "I guess you really did lose your childhood spirit. That witch must have stolen it from you, after all."

Mittens looked down and paused for a moment. "Harry!" he cried out. "You can come to get me, now." Harry quickly flew to the window and grasped Mittens with his claws.

"Gasp!" said Zoey. "That owl is going to eat the squirrel, oh no!" And, just as they were flying away, Zoey spotted Mittens' four, white paws.

"Gasp!" said Zoey, as she covered both hands over her mouth. "Could it really be them? Wait, wait!" she called out to them. But, Harry had already carried Mittens back down to the ground. They snuck behind the building to meet up with Fireball.

"Did you talk to her?" Fireball asked, impatiently. Harry and Mittens just looked at the ground.

"She couldn't hear you, could she?" asked Fireball. What the three Forest Friends didn't know, was that Zoey spotted Mittens' four, white paws and was racing down the stairs to find them.

CHAPTER SIXTEEN

Zoey's Choice

As Zoey dashed down the stairs, she couldn't help but wonder if this was all a dream. Suddenly she stopped in her tracks.

"I...I must be crazy," she said, to herself. "I must just be overtired from studying so much." To make sure, she put her hand on her forehead to see if she had a fever. It felt as cool as a cucumber, which only frustrated her more. A fever could have explained what she thought she saw. For a moment, she stood in the stairwell, wondering what she was doing. She paced back and forth, trying to diagnose her condition. Finally, she came up with a good one: homesickness.

But, she couldn't get Mittens and his white paws out of her mind. They had played together so much over the years, and she knew his markings as if she knew her own hands.

"It was him," said Zoey, as she exhaled. "But, what could he possibly be doing here? And, how did he find me?" she wondered.

She shook her head as if to shake the thoughts away and then, opened the door to finish descending the last staircase. As she crashed through the door of the dormitory, she noticed how considerably dark it was outside, now. It was going to be difficult to find Mittens if she didn't act fast.

She ran to the tree where she had first seen Harry and Mittens. Placing her hands on the bark, she looked up, searching for them.

"Hey, Zoey what are you doing?" asked a young man with dark brown hair.

"Oh...nothing," said Zoey, as she quickly whirled around and felt her cheeks warm. She tucked one of her golden curls behind her ear and looked down to the ground.

I must look very strange right now, she thought to herself. She looked up at the boy, forced a smile, and said, "It's a nice night, so I thought I would go for a walk around the campus."

He smiled and said, "Would you mind having company?"

"NO!" shouted Zoey. The boy raised his eyebrows, as he rocked back on his heels.

"I...I mean, I would rather just be alone, right now. I'm trying to clear my head before a big test tomorrow. Sorry...I hope you understand."

"Sure," said the young man, although the tone of his voice couldn't mask his disappointment.

Company was the last thing she needed. After all, she couldn't ask him to help her find a talking squirrel and owl. The very thought of this made Zoey laugh out loud. The young man raised an eyebrow in confusion.

"Oh, I'm not laughing at you," Zoey said, as she put her hands over her mouth. "I'm laughing at a...um...a funny joke someone said in class, today. Well, I'd better get going since the sun has almost set."

She swiftly turned her back to the young man and started walking away from the dormitories, towards the main building. Her eyes shifted left and right and up and down, as she scanned for any signs of Mittens and Harry. Meanwhile, just behind her dormitory stood the three Forest Friends.

"I'm afraid we have failed," said Harry. "Oh, if only I had my writing utensils, so I could have written her a message! That horrible Damen!"

"Bye, Zoey. I'll see you, tomorrow," said a boy's voice, off in the distance. The Forest Friends looked at each other and quickly peered around the corner to see Zoey walking in the opposite direction.

"Quick! There she goes!" said Fireball. Mittens took off running as fast as his legs could carry him. He caught up to her and ran around her in a circle.

"Oh!" said Zoey, as she put her hand over her mouth with surprise. "Why Mittens, it is you!" she said, as she stooped down to him. Realizing she was in the middle of her college campus, talking to a squirrel, she quickly scooped him up and ducked behind the nearest tree.

Mittens curled up in a ball, delighted to be held by his best friend. As she pet his head, she began a flurry of questions in a whispered voice.

"Mittens, how on earth did you find me? What are you doing here? Was that Harry with you?"

Mittens nodded his head. Then, he motioned with his paw behind her dormitory.

"Harry...is that where he is?" asked Zoey. Mittens started to open his mouth to answer her, but then he remembered that she couldn't hear his voice. It all seemed so strange to him since they had talked to each other, for so many years.

He thought for a moment, then climbed down her leg and motioned with his left, white paw for her to follow him. Zoey walked briskly after him and ducked behind the dormitory.

"Why Fireball and Harry!" said Zoey, as she wrapped her arms around Fireball's neck. "I just can't believe you found me, here!" she said, as Fireball nuzzled his head against her.

"We need you, Zoey," said Fireball. "We need you to come back with us to the cottage, tonight. Rorey is in danger. The witch and the wolf are coming to her house tomorrow, for dinner. She's going to try and steal Rorey's childhood spirit!"

Zoey just stared at him. She could sense something wasn't right, but she didn't know what.

"Ahhh, this is so frustrating!" said Fireball, as he stomped his hoof on the ground.

Then, he turned to Mittens and Harry. "Well, how are we supposed to get her home, if she can't even hear us?"

"I think she will follow us," said Mittens in a quiet, but yet hopeful voice.

The three friends thought for a moment, while Zoey pet Fireball.

"I've missed you all, so much," said Zoey. "I hope Matilda and all of the Forest Friends are doing well. It's been a big adjustment not seeing the cottage," she said, with her voice trailing off. "Although, I have made so many new friends here, and I'm learning a lot."

Then, Zoey thought for a moment about the cottage, and her eyes got wide.

"Rorey!" said Zoey, in an astonished voice. "Has my cousin moved in, yet? Oh, I do hope you've all had a chance to meet her. I know she will take great care of you. She will love to play all sorts of games with you, just like I did!"

But, as Zoey looked at the three Forest Friends, she saw them all lower their heads to the ground.

"Something's happened, hasn't it?" asked Zoey. "That's why you're here. You've come to tell me something. Oh, but I can't hear you, anymore!" said Zoey, as she stomped her foot on the ground.

Mittens simply nodded his head without looking up at her.

"Let's try again...one of you say something," said Zoey.

All three friends each took a turn trying to explain to Zoey about the witch and the wolf, and the great danger Rorey was in. But, all Zoey could hear was the faint music and sound of laughter coming from the nearby dormitories. By this time, it was so dark out that Zoey was having a hard time seeing the three friends.

"Wait here," she said, suddenly. "I'm going up to my room to get a few things."

The three friends looked at each other, hopeful that she would follow them home to the cottage, that night. As Zoey dashed back up the stairs to her room, she wondered what she was doing. So many thoughts were racing through her mind, and none of them were good. She sensed that something terrible was happening at the cottage, and she knew she must get there fast.

She stopped in the stairwell and took her phone out of her back pocket. Then, she began frantically scrolling through her contacts. She would find her aunt and uncle's phone number and call them to make sure everything at the cottage was alright. She found the number:

Aunt Sherry & Uncle Tim
Home
(315) 555-2714

She hit the call button and held her breath. One ring. Then a voicemail: "Hi, you've reached Sherry and Tim. I'm sorry we can't come to the phone right now, but if you..."

"Ugh, they must already be asleep," said Zoey, as she tilted her head back and exhaled loudly. She checked the time on her phone. She knew the last bus had already left the station, and none of her friends had a car reliable enough to drive more than just a few miles. She thought about calling her parents, but they would just worry that she was homesick for the cottage. And surely, she wouldn't be able to explain that the Forest Friends were standing outside of her dormitory! They might commit her if she did. Her parents would often worry about how much she talked to the animals, especially as she got older. She didn't want to cause them any more worry. After all, it's cute and charming when a five-year-old can hear animals, but not so much when you're almost eighteen.

There was no other choice, but to trust her friends, and her instincts, and follow them into the forest. She got to the top of the stairs and flung open the door to her room. Thank goodness her roommate was not back from the dining hall yet. She didn't want to have to answer any questions.

There on her bed was her pink backpack. She dumped out her schoolbooks, notebook, and pens. Then, she quickly stuffed it with warm clothes, a few snacks, a flashlight, and her water bottle.

"I should let someone know where I am," she said. She wrote a note to her roommate and placed it on her desk.

Dear Remy,

I had to go home for an emergency. Don't worry. I'll be fine and will be back, as soon as I can.

Love,

Zoey

She slung the backpack over her shoulder and ran down the stairs as fast as her feet would carry her. When she got back to the Forest Friends, she looked at them and nodded.

"Well, you seem to know the way, so I'll follow you." And without another word, the four friends set out into the now dark sky, under the bright full moon.

CHAPTER SEVENTEEN

The Wolf Is Waiting

Thankfully for the friends, the full moon acted as a street-light in the now pitch-black sky. Harry glided silently above them. Fireball walked a couple of paces in front of Zoey to lead the way, while Mittens was perfectly content tucked into the front of Zoey's zipped up pink jacket. For the first few moments of the walk, no one said anything until they reached a fence that they needed to climb over.

Zoey hesitated for a moment. Just beyond the fence, the trees thickened and they were heading into the darkness of the forest. She reached inside her backpack and took out her flashlight. Then, Fireball, with his strength and grace, took one swift leap over the fence. Zoey, on the other hand, was small enough to tuck herself between the slats.

"You never cease to amaze me," Zoey said, as she smiled at Fireball. This made Fireball smile. He used to love showing off his running and jumping skills, to the amazement of the young girl with golden curls.

As they continued to walk, Zoey couldn't help but think of the terrible things, which may be happening at the cottage. She hoped she was overreacting, but in her heart, she knew that the Forest Friends were there to warn her about some great danger. And, deep down she felt that it had something to do with the witch and the wolf. At the very thought of them, she began to twist and twirl one of her golden curls around her finger, as they walked into the moonlit forest. The friends walked silently, for what seemed to Zoey, like an eternity.

"Wait, I need to rest for a minute," said Zoey, as she sunk to the ground. She slipped her heavy backpack off her shoulders and let it crash to the forest floor.

Harry made a U-turn in the sky and gently floated down to the ground, to rest with them. Fireball trotted over towards Zoey, as she got her water bottle out of her backpack. It occurred to the Forest Friends that they, too, were thirsty and getting quite hungry.

As she drank her water, she realized there were peanut butter crackers in her bag...Mittens' favorite treat. She pulled out the crackers and shook the bag in front of Mittens to get his attention. His eyes widened, as he climbed out of her jacket. She laughed as she fed him.

"I know you're here because something is wrong," sighed Zoey. "But I can't help but be happy at this moment. I've missed you all, more than you can know." But, the Forest Friends did know, all too well, the heartbreak of saying goodbye to someone they loved.

As she finished her last cracker, her eyes began to close, and she leaned up against Fireball.

"Fireball, I think she's falling asleep!" shouted Mittens.

"Here, let's get her to climb on me, so she won't have to walk, anymore," said Fireball. "We don't have much time to rest. We've got to get back to the cottage before the sun sets tomorrow."

Fireball gently pressed his head against Zoey's shoulder to wake her up. She opened her eyes as he lowered his body so that she could climb on him. She slung her backpack over her shoulder and hopped up. Then, she scooped up Mittens and gently placed him back in her jacket pocket.

They walked and walked, descending deeper and deeper into the forest. What the friends didn't know, was that Damen had spotted them. As they approached a small creek, he stepped out of the darkness. The moonlight seemed to dance off of his glistening teeth.

"Hello, my dear Zoey," said Damen, with a crooked smile. "I wondered if you'd make it in time, for our little party."

"Damen!" shouted Zoey. One moment ago, she was almost asleep. Now, she was as awake as if someone had thrown a bucket of ice water on her head.

"See, you didn't stop us from bringing her back!" said Mittens, as he stuck his tongue out at the wolf.

"Yes, I can see that, Mittens," said Damen, as his green eyes suddenly flashed red. "But I do wonder...can she really hear you?" He sauntered towards them, walking slowly around the friends in a circle.

"It doesn't matter anymore, Damen, because she's going to stop Esmerelda, tomorrow!" shouted Fireball.

"If she makes it," said Damen. "It is still an awfully long walk, and she might encounter dangerous creatures along the way."

"You mean like you?" said Fireball, as he took a step towards Damen.

Zoey patted Fireball on the head and said, "It's ok, boy, let's turn back." She couldn't hear them, but Damen's dark energy hung around them, like a vulture feeding off of a carcass.

"You see?" said Damen, with a smile. "She must sense that danger is ahead. Don't you want to protect your friend?" he asked, as he glided his rough tongue along the top row of his long, yellow teeth.

Just then, a cold wind gust blew. It sent brown, dead leaves swirling quickly around them, like a tornado. The wind was so loud and strong, that Zoey had to lean forward and loop her arms around Fireball's neck, to keep from falling over. Her golden curls flew wildly around her head, from the force of the wind.

"You know, on second thought, I think I'll save some room for you three, for dessert tomorrow," shouted Damen over the wind.

"I'm sure Esmerelda will appreciate that I kept you alive long enough so that she could say goodbye to you, first."

"Damen, I'm warning you!" yelled Fireball.

But, before he knew it, the wind died down and the dead, brown leaves fell around them in a circle. All that was left of Damen were his big, red paw prints.

"This...this is not good," shivered Mittens, who had burrowed down further into Zoey's jacket.

"My goodness, what was that all about?" asked Zoey. The Forest Friends forgot, for a moment, that Zoey couldn't hear their conversation.

"Fireball, he's going to tell Esmerelda about Zoey returning!" cried out Mittens. "She's going to try and stop us!"

"Let her come," said Fireball. "I want to repay her for what she did to my Mother and me."

CHAPTER EIGHTEEN

The Wolf's Lie

As the sun began to rise over the cottage on a peaceful morning, no one inside the house had any idea of the danger that encircled them in the forest. The birds chirped their cheerful morning songs, to gently wake up the world. Papa was awake and decided to make the family a big breakfast. They had many house chores to do that day, to get ready for the evening's dinner plans. Little did they know, the evil intentions of Esmerelda.

Papa placed thick slabs of bacon into the frying pan and poured himself a piping hot cup of coffee. Like magic, the delicious aromas woke everyone else up in the cottage. It was as if the different scents knocked on everyone's door, telling them that it was morning. Chihuahua Lola was the first to rise and decided to play guard dog, to make sure nothing happened to the bacon. This was a very serious job, after all.

"Mommy," said Rorey, as she and Ryann came out to the kitchen.

"What is it, honey?" asked Ryann.

"Can Rocky come over again, today?" she asked.

"He can come over whenever he wants to," smiled Ryann, as she gently stroked Rorey's dark curls.

"I'm making a big breakfast, so eat up, this morning," said Papa, as he flipped over the bacon that was sizzling on the stove. "We have boxes to sort through and house cleaning before our barbeque, this evening. We're all going to need our energy."

"Yawn," said Ryann, as she poured herself a cup of coffee. "Oh, is that tonight?" sighed Ryann, as she rubbed her eyes.

"Yes," laughed Papa. "What's the matter?"

"I'm not sure I like Esmerelda," snorted Ryann.

"Well, then tonight is the perfect chance to get to know her," said Papa.

"Rocky doesn't like her," said Ryann.

"Rocky doesn't like, who?" asked Nana, as she walked around the corner in her house robe and fuzzy, pink slippers.

"Esmerelda," said Ryann.

"Oh, let's not start that again," said Nana, as she blew her golden bangs up and out of her blue eyes. "You two just got off on the wrong foot. I'm sure you'll think differently about her, after tonight."

Ding-dong!

Rorey whirled around to see who it was, hopeful that it was her friend, Rocky.

"It looks like Rocky and Heather," said Ryann, and she got up to answer the door.

"Good Morning," said Heather, as she handed Ryann a warm, bread pan.

"What's this?" said Ryann. "It smells so good!"

"It's banana bread," said Heather.

"I love banana bread!" said Papa, as he leaned around the corner to wave at Heather. "Why don't you all come to our barbeque, tonight?" said Papa.

"Oh yes, you must!" said Nana, as she clasped her hands together. "Feel free to invite the other neighbors, as well. I know we don't have many out here in the forest, but still," laughed Nana.

"That sounds great!" said Heather.

"Hi, Rocky!" said Rorey, as she peeked around her mom, with a smile.

"Hi, Rorey!" smiled Rocky. "Do you want to play outside with me?"

"Ya!" shouted Rorey.

"Ahem. Hold on there, Ro-Ro," said Ryann. "First you have to finish all of your breakfast, ok?" Rorey nodded and climbed up onto one of the wooden kitchen chairs.

"Heather, I made extra in the hopes that you two would stop by," said Papa. "I hope you're hungry."

Heather laughed and said, "I think you've fed us breakfast every day since you've moved in."

"We're neighbors, so let's just make this a new tradition," smiled Papa, as he flipped a pancake through the air, much to Rocky's amusement.

They gathered around the small kitchen table laughing, eating, and talking about all the chores they were going to do that day, to get ready for the barbeque. Heather offered to stay and help so that Rocky and Rorey could play together. Meanwhile, the basset hounds were fast asleep under the kitchen table, but not Chihuahua Lola. She was still conducting her bacon-guarding duty, and she knew that curling up under Rorey's chair offered her the best opportunity to "clean up" any of the food bits that happened to hit the floor. This too was a duty she took quite seriously. It was such exhausting work, she planned to spend the rest of the day napping in her little pink bed.

As they ate breakfast, the Forest Friends peered through the back window of the cottage, to hear what they were saying.

"What time is the dinner?" asked Nosey Rosey.

"Shhh, I can't hear what they're saying!" hissed Gary.

"Oh, you're so cute when you get angry!" said Nosey Rosey, as she purred and batted her eyes at Gary.

Meanwhile, Penney was trying to keep her fox kits quiet and calm, so she could listen in, too. Matilda watched from a distance. Then, she looked up at the sky and closed her eyes.

"I do hope they make it in time," she whispered to herself. She could feel in her heart that Zoey would be coming home, today. "Zoey, we need you," she said. Then, she opened her eyes and looked back at the cottage. She knew that to stop Esmerelda from stealing Rorey's childhood spirit, that they needed a plan. With Harry gone, Matilda knew she needed to summon his Head Messenger, Ansel, to get an important message out to the Forest Friends.

"Ansel!" she called out while standing underneath his tree. He came out of his little wooden, arch-shaped tree house and glided gracefully to the ground, with his messenger bag ready.

"Ansel, I need you to spread the news. Have the Forest Friends meet in Deer Valley, before the sun sets over the cottage. I will give further instruction there."

"Yes, Matilda," said Ansel, as he wrote down the message on the tree bark with the tip of his wing. Then, with two flaps of his wings, he soared into the sky. Within moments, dozens and dozens of owls were out in full force, dropping the tree bark messages throughout the forest.

"Matilda, Matilda!" gasped Nosey Rosey and Penney, as they came running towards her. "We just heard that Rorey and Rocky are coming outside to play, soon," said Nosey Rosey. "Maybe we can get them to hear us, today!"

Matilda smiled. "Yes, we should try again, shouldn't we?"

"Oh, I don't know if that's such a good idea," said a low voice from behind them.

Matilda continued to stare straight forward, as she knew the voice, all too well.

"I'm just not so sure the little girl's Mommy will want her to play outside, with such a big and scary dog in the front yard," said Damen.

"Damen, you get out of here!" said Penney, in a high-pitched voice.

"Who are you talking to, you little mutt?" snapped Damen. "I could eat you for breakfast and still have room for your little pups!" he snapped once more, showing his mighty jaws.

"Penney, why don't you and the others go back to the cottage and stand guard there," said Matilda.

Penney looked at her, still in shock from Damen. "But...but Matilda," she said, as her voice quivered.

"It's alright. I'll be fine here," said Matilda.

Damen broke out into laughter. "You know, Esmerelda has the most beautiful flowers for Rorey. It won't be long now before she wins her trust. It's too bad you didn't get a chance to get to know Rorey before...well...you know. Oh, what a pity. You've already lost your Zoey, and tonight, you'll lose Rorey, too."

Matilda closed her eyes and looked up towards the sky.

Damen snorted. "Well, there's no use in me standing around here by you, Matilda. I think I'll go for a nice leisurely stroll, around the cottage."

Creeeak!

The front screen door flew open, as Rorey and Rocky dashed off the front porch into the yard.

"Hey, you two stay where we can see you," said Ryann, as she came out onto the front porch, holding her white coffee mug. Just then, she spotted Damen.

"Rorey! Rocky! Come back in here, right now!" she yelled frantically. With a loud *smash*, the coffee mug she was holding shattered when it hit the ground. Black liquid dripped down the sidewalk behind her, as she dashed into the front yard. Damen delighted at this and began to trot towards them with a low growl. Ryann scooped up Rorey, grabbed Rocky by the hand, and sprinted back towards the cottage. With that, they heard the door slam shut and the sound of the deadbolt locking.

"Well, I guess my work here is done, for now," said Damen. "I do hope to see you at tonight's little festivities, Matilda. Oh, and don't worry about your little guests coming. I saw them in the forest last night, and well...I'm sorry to tell you this...but an awful creature got to them."

"I don't believe you, Damen," said Matilda, as she looked him deep in the eyes. She could tell he was lying because his green eyes flashed red.

"Suit yourself," said Damen. As he turned away, he kicked up a cloud of dirt into Matilda's face, with one of his giant paws.

As he meandered off into the forest, Matilda shook the dust and dirt from her head. But, she couldn't help but smile. Zoey must be on her way, she thought to herself. Damen's lie was proof that he couldn't stop them.

Just then, Penney, Nosey Rosey, Gary, and Zoro came over to Matilda. They were so distraught about Damen chasing the children back into the cottage.

"Oh Matilda, what do we do now?" cried Nosey Rosey. "Now, they won't let them come outside to play, and we won't be able to talk to them and warn them about Esmerelda!"

"It's alright, my dear friends," said Matilda. "Zoey is coming."

CHAPTER NINETEEN

What Rocky Knows

"**M**ommy, what's wrong?" asked Rorey, when they were back inside the cottage. Her eyebrows were furrowed, as she twirled one of her dark curls around her finger. Even though she looked nothing like Zoey, this habit was a family trait they happened to share. Ryann was still leaning against the front door. She clutched the door's handle with her right hand and had her other hand placed over her thumping heart.

"Alright, take deep breaths," said Nana, as she gently rubbed Ryann's back.

"I'm…I'm alright, now," said Ryann, as she tried to slow down her breathing.

Ricky came around the corner, with the two basset hounds trailing right behind him. He held out his hand to Ryann and helped guide her over to one of the kitchen chairs.

"Here, drink some water," he said, as he handed her a glass. The basset hounds and Chihuahua Lola could sense the distress in the air. They stood in a line staring out the front window as if they were the Queen of England's guards in front of Buckingham Palace. The hair on the backs of their necks stood on end.

As Ryann reached for the glass, Rocky and Rorey noticed how her hands shook.

"What did you see that frightened you, so badly?" asked Papa.

The entire family was gathered around the kitchen table, as she told them what she saw. It was a big...no...no...a GIANT gray wolf, with piercing green eyes and yellow fangs, which dripped with saliva.

"That's Damen," said Rocky. Every head in the house turned towards Rocky.

"Rocky, what do you mean?" asked Heather. "How do you know his name?"

"That's Esmerelda's dog," he said, as he looked towards the ground.

Ring Ring!

They all looked towards Nana's cell phone, which was singing a little tune.

"Oh, now who could that be?" she huffed, as she walked over to the kitchen counter and picked up the phone. "Hello? Yes? Oh yes, hello Esmerelda," said Nana. Now, every head in the house turned to look towards Nana. "No, please don't worry about bringing anything, for tonight. Yes, yes that's very sweet of you, but you are our guest, and we have more than enough food." There was a slight pause, as Nana listened to Esmerelda on the other end. "Alright, we will see you, then. Yes, we are looking forward to it, too. Goodbye."

"Rocky, how could that giant bbb...beast be Esmerelda's dog?" asked Ryann.

Rocky shrugged his shoulders and said, "He's always at her cottage." Then he thought for a moment, smiled at Nana and Papa, and asked, "Can I have some more pancakes?"

"Yes, of course, you can, sweetheart," said Nana, as she rushed off to the kitchen to get him more pancakes.

"Rocky, forget about the pancakes," said Heather. "How do you know about Esmerelda's dog?"

"Dog...that is not a dog!" said Ryann, with a panicked laugh. "That is a wolf...a wild and horrible creature! What is she doing with a wolf for a pet?"

Nana put a plate full of pancakes in front of Rocky, as he smiled big and said, "Thank you...I sure do looove pancakes!"

Heather rolled her eyes and said, "Rocky, I want to know how you know about Esmerelda and her...dog."

"Because I saw him, one time. Daddy and I went for a walk in the woods, and we saw a scary house with a lady outside. She was wearing this scary red dress, and it looked like blood. She was shouting 'Damen, Damen!' Then, Daddy and I saw the big scary dog running around her front yard. Daddy talked to Esmerelda, for a couple of minutes. She asked me if I wanted to pick wildflowers with her to surprise Mommy, but I didn't want to. I was too scared of her dog."

"Mom, you must tell her to keep that creature contained in her yard!" said Ryann, as she whirled around in her chair and stared at Nana.

"Yes, I will call her back," said Nana. "Now listen, let's not get all worked up about this, for tonight. Let's just focus on our chores and try and have a pleasant evening, ok?"

Ryann folded her arms. "I don't like that woman," she said quietly to herself.

"Bark, bark, bark!" they heard.

This caused Ryann to jump out of her chair. The basset hounds were tilting their heads back and baying. This sent Chihuahua Lola into a high-pitched bark. She held her head back in the air, trying with all her might, to be out heard by the basset hounds.

"Is he back, again?" asked Ryann, as she rushed over and peered out the window with both hands gripping the curtains.

"Oh, for heaven's sake, it's just a cat," said Nana, as she looked out the window.

"Come here, you three," said Papa in a deep voice, as he sat in one of the dark green living room recliners. He clapped his hands together, to signal for the dogs to come to him. All three instantly ran to Papa, with their tails wagging and heads down as if to say they were sorry for causing such a raucous over a silly little cat.

"Chihuahua Lola, it's ok," said Rorey.

Lola turned and came running towards Rorey. Then she stood up on her hind legs and licked her nose. This always made Rorey giggle.

"Well, I suppose I should take a shower," said Ryann. "Rorey, don't go outside without my permission, ok?"

"OK, Mommy," said Rorey.

So, Rorey and Rocky played their usual game of hide and seek indoors on this day.

CHAPTER TWENTY

Zoey's Dream

"Ahhh...Ahhh...Achoo!" sneezed Mittens, as they walked through the forest.

"Poor Mittens," said Zoey. "I see your allergies are no better," she said, as she gave his head a little rub...much to his delight. "Oh, I need to stop and rest again," she said, as she slung the backpack off from her shoulders and dropped it to the mossy forest floor. "I think I have just enough food to last us until we get to the cottage," she said, as she rummaged through the largest pocket of her backpack.

Fireball gently kicked an acorn towards Mittens, who had climbed out of Zoey's pocket. He hopped down to retrieve his treat, as Harry gently glided back down, softly landing on the forest floor. As the four friends rested and ate, Zoey began to wonder what she was walking into. But, after seeing Damen, she knew for sure Esmerelda had something to do with this. The very thought of her name sent chills down her spine. She shivered, even though it was the middle of a warm day.

When she had finished the last bits of peanut butter crackers, she closed her eyes and rested against Fireball, who stood firm and looked around for any sign of the witch or the wolf. The moment Zoey closed her eyes, she could see Esmerelda's beautiful, twinkling white dress glowing against the green forest's backdrop. Zoey could still hear the witch's syrupy sweet, yet still cold voice even after all these years:

"Zoey, would you like to pick wildflowers with me?"

Then Zoey shivered again, as she began to think about that awful day when Damen attacked Matilda and had broken her leg. She will never forget the sound of Matilda's voice, and how she had saved her from Damen. After the witch and the wolf were gone, Zoey went out to help Matilda, for she was so worried about her leg. She snuck some bandages and a clean, wet cloth from the cottage, and hid them in her sand bucket, so her parents wouldn't ask what she was doing. Zoey had found poor Matilda laying down, just inside the tree line. Then, she cleaned and bandaged her broken leg.

It had been years since Zoey thought of that day. It always brought back so many memories that she tried to push away. It was too difficult for her to think about the witch and the wolf. They terrified her to this very day.

As Zoey leaned up against Fireball, she began to drift off. They had been walking for such a long time. She fought to keep her eyes open but to no avail. And, as she drifted off to sleep, Zoey's dream took her back to that fateful day of her childhood. A day that would change everything.

CHAPTER TWENTY-ONE

Esmerelda and the Old Woman

As she slept against Fireball, Zoey tried to fight off the memories of her childhood with Damen and the witch. But this time, her dream would take her back to the day when she was five years old...

"You saved me," little Zoey had said to Matilda. "I didn't know you could talk."

Matilda smiled. "I'm so glad you heard my voice. I've been talking to you every day, hoping that one day you would hear me."

Zoey paused for a moment. "Why did the wolf bite you?" she asked.

"The wolf is Esmerelda's pet," said Matilda. "And, Esmerelda is a witch with terrible powers. You must never trust her."

And so, Matilda began to tell Zoey about her awful sister and her evil intentions.

"She was going to steal my heart?" asked Zoey.

"Yes, my dear," said Matilda. "You see, she needs *your* heart. For locked away deep inside every heart, there lives a childhood spirit. Since most adults have lost their childhood spirit, Esmerelda needs the warmth and wonder that can only be found in the heart of a child."

The more Matilda told Zoey about the witch, the closer Zoey moved to her, until she had gently leaned up against her.

"Every year, she loses a little more of her terrible powers," Matilda said. "Your childhood spirit is the only thing that will keep her icy heart beating. Esmerelda wants to stay a witch for all eternity. And, if she succeeds, I'm afraid she will turn the forest into winter, forever."

As little Zoey dabbed Matilda's leg with the cloth, Matilda told her the story of her jealous and evil sister, who had turned her and Fireball into deer.

"But why, Matilda?" asked Zoey, with the innocence of a five-year-old child. "Why does Esmerelda want to be a witch?"

"My sister grew very jealous and bitter," said Matilda. "She is a few years younger than me, and I always felt very protective of her, but when I moved out of the cottage and went to school to study ballet, she and I became more distant. A few years later, I was married. A year after that, I had Jax," said Matilda, with a smile. "When Jax was born, she became more withdrawn from the family. He was taking up all of the attention. She would often miss important moments like birthday parties and Christmas dinners. My parents and I became more worried about her. She began sneaking off into the forest for hours and would come home long after the sun had set. She refused to tell anyone where she had been, or what she had been up to. One day, I decided to follow her. I hid behind the trees, chasing her as quietly as I could. I didn't understand what she was doing. She had a piece of paper in one hand and a basket in the other and would place things into it. First a toad. Then a mushroom. Then a wild berry. She would check the list as she went. It was as if she were on a scavenger hunt."

"Where was she going?" asked Zoey.

"Well, after she had gathered many things from the forest, she stopped in front of a large cave. Then, an old woman walked out of the darkness of the cave. She wore a black cloak that covered her head."

"Have you brought me the items?" asked the old woman to Esmerelda, who was but sixteen at the time.

"Yes, your Excellency," said Esmerelda, as she presented the basket to the old woman and kneeled at her feet.

The old woman rummaged through the basket.

"Good...very good," she said to Esmerelda. "Now, it's time for you to pass the final test," said the old woman.

"But...but, I thought this was the final test?" asked Esmerelda, with confusion.

"I thought I told you to address me properly!" yelled the old woman. Then, she pulled a slender, white wand from the front pocket of her cloak, and pointed it straight at Esmerelda. Then, she pointed it at a nearby boulder that was the size of a small car. With the faintest flick of her wrist, the boulder instantly turned to ice and shattered into bits.

"I'm...I'm sorry, your Excellency," said Esmerelda, as she bowed before her.

"That's better," said the old woman. "Now, I can make you the most powerful creature in this forest. I have already taught you a great many spells, haven't I?" asked the old woman.

"Yes, your Excellency," said Esmerelda.

"But, there is one final thing you must do for me before you can receive your wand. You must bring me the heart of a child," said the old woman.

"What?" asked Esmerelda.

"I need the heart of a child, to keep my powers," said the old woman. "Bring me the heart of a child, and I will make you the most powerful witch this forest has ever seen."

"But how do I..." asked Esmerelda, as her voice trailed off.

"Oh, there are many ways," the old woman cackled. Then, she rubbed the end of the wand between two of her long, boney fingers. "Many, many ways. You're a clever girl—trick the child into following you here. I will show you how to take a childhood spirit. Now go!"

Esmerelda took off running into the forest. Matilda, in shock of what she had just seen and heard, chased after her sister into the forest.

"Esmerelda, stop!" cried out Matilda.

Esmerelda turned around suddenly. She was horrified to find her sister standing there.

"Matilda, what are you doing here?" she yelled, angrily. "Did you follow me?"

"Yes, we've all been so worried about you," said Matilda. "And, now I see we have a reason to be worried!"

Matilda reached for Esmerelda's hand, but she swatted it away like a pesky mosquito.

"Worried about me?" laughed Esmerelda. "Please! All you and anyone talk about is that son of yours," she snapped.

"You're not actually thinking about bringing a child to that old woman, are you?" asked Matilda.

"Hmmph. Maybe I should bring her Jax," said Esmerelda, as she folded her arms.

"You don't mean that," said Matilda.

"Look, don't pretend to suddenly care about me," said Esmerelda. "You've chosen your life. And, I've chosen mine." Then, she spun around and dashed through the forest as fast as her feet would carry her.

"No, stop!" cried out Matilda.

But, she couldn't keep up with her sister. Somewhere in the thickness of the forest, she had lost her. And in fact, she was now lost herself. The sun was beginning to lower in the sky, and she began to grow more frightened. She had nothing with her, and no one, except Esmerelda, knew where she was.

And so poor Matilda wandered around the forest like a lost lamb for days. She was tired, hungry, and thirsty. Then, as she stopped at a creek for a drink of water, she could hear the sounds of faint voices and dogs barking.

She began to run towards the sounds, but she was so weak that she tripped over a tree root. Laying on the ground, she held on to her ankle, which she knew was sprained. As she lay there waiting for someone to find her, she saw Esmerelda walking towards her.

In her hand, she held a long, slender wand. It was the same one that the old woman had. Then, without so much as a word, she pointed it at Matilda. Her once sparkling blue eyes were now icy—a color Matilda didn't recognize in her sister's eyes.

"Mommy!" she suddenly heard Jax yell.

Matilda quickly turned to see her son, a young boy with sandy-brown hair, running towards her. Off in the distance, she could see the people with the search dogs. Then she watched, as Esmerelda turned and pointed the wand at Jax.

"No!" screamed Matilda. But, instead of turning Jax to ice, she watched, as her son was instantly transformed into a full-grown, beautiful buck.

Then, Esmerelda spun around and pointed the wand at Matilda.

"You should thank me for this," said Esmerelda, as her icy eyes flickered.

And, those were the last words Matilda heard before she was transformed into a deer.

CHAPTER TWENTY-TWO

Winter *Is* Coming

Suddenly, Zoey's eyes opened. The dream had felt so real and just like it had happened yesterday. She was still leaning up against Fireball, but now the whole forest seemed to be swaying. She had not thought about that day for so long. Now she grew dizzy, as a million questions raced through her head.

Was it possible that Esmerelda had already stolen the childhood spirit from her heart? Zoey placed her hand on her heart as if to search for it. Is this why she couldn't hear the Forest Friends, anymore? Was any of it even real? Had she made it up when she was a child? Was Esmerelda trying to steal Rorey's heart and childhood spirit? Even if this were all true, would anyone believe her?

"Ohhh!" she cried out, as she tried to stand. Then, she fell to her knees and put her head into her hands. She sobbed and sobbed, not sure of what to do, or what to believe. She didn't even know why she was here in the middle of the forest when she should be at university taking her test.

"Fireball, what do we do?" cried Mittens. His gray tail twitched back and forth.

"Just let her be for a few moments," said Fireball.

"Wait...I know...she loves tricks," said Mittens. "I'll do one of her favorite tricks, to make her laugh."

Then, Mittens twitched his tail back and forth, as he raced around the forest, collecting as many acorns as he could. He ran back and parked himself right in front of Zoey. He waved his tiny, white paws to get her attention. Then, he stuffed as many acorns into his mouth as he could.

Zoey watched with tears still streaming down her face. Her sobs began to quiet, as she started to giggle in disbelief at Mittens, who now had so many acorns stuffed in his mouth, that he could no longer close it.

"Why Mittens, you still remember my favorite trick," she laughed. Then, a cold, harsh wind shot out of the forest like a cannon and swirled leaves all around them. This, of course, made Mittens sneeze every last acorn out of his mouth.

Zoey stood up and blinked the last remaining tears from her eyes.

"Wait a minute," she said, as she looked up into the forest trees. "It's barely autumn, and at least half of the leaves have already fallen from the trees."

She looked around trying to understand why piles of brown, dead leaves covered the forest floor. They were now covering her ankles. Something wasn't right. Then, she remembered what Matilda had said that fateful day:

"And, if she succeeds, my dear...I'm afraid she will turn the forest into winter, forever."

And with that, Zoey realized why the Forest Friends came to get her. She had to save the forest from the witch.

"This must be real," said Zoey. "I'm...I'm not going crazy. Winter is coming early, and it's Esmerelda!" she said. Then she looked at Fireball, Mittens, and Harry with big, wide eyes. "And, you three know about it...and, you need my help!"

The Forest Friend's mouths dropped open with shock. They always knew Zoey was a clever girl, but she always had a way of surprising them with her smarts. They looked at her, then at each other, and then back at her. They didn't know what to say, and since Zoey probably couldn't hear them anyway, they simply nodded.

"Well, then what are we waiting for...let's go home!" yelled Zoey. She grabbed her backpack, slung it back over her shoulders, and took off running deeper into the forest.

Fireball looked at Mittens and smiled. "I think we have our little Zoey back," he said.

And with that, Harry took to the sky, and Mittens climbed on Fireball's antlers, as he galloped after Zoey.

CHAPTER TWENTY-THREE

Home at Last

"La da dee...la da doo..." sang Papa, as he scrubbed and scrubbed the barbeque grill, getting ready for the evening's dinner. He loved to grill because it was the only time Nana let him wear his green apron and tall chef's hat. Meanwhile, Nana was busying herself with setting up the picnic table. She hummed to herself, as she draped a white tablecloth over the picnic table. Then, she adorned it with fresh flowers and white tea candles in mason jars, which danced like lightning bugs in the now fading sunlight. As she checked her watch, she couldn't help but notice how much more quickly the light was chased away by the darkness of the thick forest walls.

"Well, I'm going to get the food ready, now," said Papa, as he headed into the cottage. Moments later, he came out with a large, silver tray piled high with hamburgers, hotdogs, veggie kabobs, and corn on the cob. As he began to grill, the delicious aromas and smoke began to gently swirl and dance around the forest.

Inside the cottage, Rorey stood at the bottom of the stairs, calling her mom.

"Mommy, can I go outside with Nana and Papa? I want to see Sniffles!" said Rorey.

"Mom, can I go outside, too?" pleaded Rocky to Heather.

As Ryann came down the stairs, she looked out the window.

"Heather, did my Mom call Esmerelda?" she asked.

"Yes, she did," said Heather. "She told her that Damen was in the yard and frightened us, and to make sure he stays in her yard," she said.

"Good," said Ryann, as she folded her arms.

As she looked down at Rorey and Rocky, she couldn't help but smile at their big, pleading eyes.

"Oh, alright," said Ryann. "But, you must stay where we can see you, at all times," she said.

"Yay!" yelled Rorey and Rocky, as they jumped up and down.

As they came crashing through the back door, Nana called to them.

"Oh good, just the helpers I needed!" said Nana.

Rorey and Rocky ran to her, each thrilled that they could help with tonight's party plans. So, she showed them how to put napkins on everyone's placemat.

Meanwhile, as the sun set over the cottage, every Forest Friend took their usual place in Deer Valley. Matilda slowly limped to her tree stump, to address the chattering crowd.

"My dear friends," she began softly. "Our dearest Zoey will be here shortly." At the sound of this, the entire forest let out a cheer.

"But, we must help her stop Esmerelda and Damen," she said sternly. "We cannot allow Esmerelda or Damen to get close to Rorey. We must do whatever it takes." The Forest Friends looked around at each other and nodded. They were all determined to stop the evil witch from harming Rorey.

"Matilda, Matilda!" called a voice from the sky. All of the Forest Friends looked up to see Ansel soaring above them. His shadow passed over Matilda's tree stump, as he landed in front of her. "I've spotted them!"

"Who...who have you spotted, Ansel?" eagerly asked Matilda.

"Harry! Did you know that he made it to Zoey's university, without the tree bark message?"

The Forest Friends let out a gasp.

"Oh no, without the tree bark message, Zoey won't know that we need her!" cried out Nosey Rosey.

"But, that's just it!" said Ansel.

"Zoey is with him, Fireball, and Mittens! They aren't more than a mile from the cottage!"

At the sound of this, Matilda galloped and with two quick hops, disappeared into the forest.

"Well, what are we waiting for?" cried out Zoro. "Let's all go!"

And with that, all of the Forest Friends went into a sprint towards the tree line. Every squirrel, fox, cat, bird, deer, possum, and turtle rushed to be one of the first to see their dear friend, Zoey.

As Zoey, Mittens, and Fireball approached the cottage, Zoey recognized a tree that she had carved on when she was a young girl. She rushed over to it and placed her hands on the tree. In the tree, she had carved out her initials "ZB." Next to the initials were a little heart, a carving of a deer with a broken leg, and a squirrel.

"I'm home," she said, as she wrapped her arms around the tree and closed her eyes, with a smile.

When she opened her eyes, she saw Matilda standing not far from the tree, on top of a small hill. The sunlight filtered through the trees, casting a majestic glow around her.

"Matilda!" said Zoey, as her eyes widened.

Just then, she heard a loud *Snap!* Zoey whirled around, to see Damen standing just inches behind her. He had crushed a twig underneath one of his enormous paws.

"Welcome home, dear Zoey!" said Damen. "But I'm afraid your journey will end right here."

Zoey just stared at him in disbelief, wondering if she should run, climb a tree, or play dead.

"Oh, that's right," said Damen. "I keep forgetting that you can't hear me, anymore. Since you seem to have lost your childhood spirit, perhaps I should just let you go. But then again, you could warn Rorey and her family about Esmerelda, and we just can't have that, can we?" snarled Damen.

"Zoey, run!" shouted Matilda.

And, with those same words, Zoey was five years old again. She heard Matilda's voice, just as clearly as she had that first day when Damen tried to attack her. Zoey spun back around towards Matilda.

"I...I heard you," she said. And, just like when she was five, Zoey did as Matilda said. She ran towards home.

CHAPTER TWENTY-FOUR

Zoey and the Wolf

Zoey broke through the trees and made it to the cottage's front yard, just as the Forest Friends stampeded towards her. She covered her hand over her mouth to keep from screaming and closed her eyes, as she felt the rushing wind of the animals while they ran past her. Then the Forest Friends formed a protective circle around Zoey. This stopped Damen in his tracks.

"Ready, friends?" yelled out Penney. "Attack!"

And with that, all of the Forest Friends rushed towards Damen. The owls swooped in from above, dropping rocks on his head. The squirrels climbed on his back, as they nipped and clawed their way through his thick, mangled fur. Mittens, himself, got in on the fun by throwing an acorn at Damen's head.

Damen gave a quick shake and threw all of the squirrels off of him, at once. Then, with one giant leap, he lunged towards Zoey. He managed to grab her shoelace with the tips of his teeth.

"No!" cried out Matilda, as she used her back legs to give Damen one strong kick to his side. This caused Damen to release Zoey's shoe from his mighty jaws. Zoey scrambled away, quickly stood up, and continued to run. This enraged him.

"Ahhhh!" the wolf yelled at Matilda, as his eyes flashed red. "I will finish you off this time, Matilda!" yelled Damen, as he whirled around to face her.

Zoey spun around to see Damen skulking his way towards Matilda, ready to pounce.

"Matilda!" cried out Zoey. She reached for a large tree limb that had fallen. It was heavy and hard for her to carry, but all she could think about was saving her best friend. She rushed towards Damen, lifted the large branch high over her head, and slammed the tree limb onto his back. Damen crashed to the ground and howled in pain.

Then, he spun around again to face Zoey, who was trembling from head to toe. He panted, dug his sharp claws deep into the earth, and let out a howl that shook the birds from the trees.

As she watched the wolf, Zoey realized that she had two choices: run away from Damen now and for the rest of her life, or defeat him. "If I could get him to follow me, I could lead him towards the edge of the bluff," Zoey said to herself. She grasped the tree branch tighter in her hand.

"Hey, Damen, what's the matter?" Zoey taunted him, though her voice still shook. "You can't ever seem to catch me. Not even when I was five." She saw the flash of red in his eyes.

This caused Damen to let out a low growl. His entire body shook, as he lifted his head to the sky and let out another wailing howl. Zoey turned a sharp right, away from the cottage she was so desperate to see, and ran towards the edge of the bluff that overlooked the Mississippi River. This is where she would always go when she needed to think or to escape her world. But on this evening, the bluff would serve a very different purpose. She was going there to lead Damen to his demise.

As she ran, the thick tree branches scraped against her cheeks like claws reaching for her. The stinging pain made her eyes tear up, but she never felt more alive. A new surge of strength welled up from somewhere deep inside of her. How freeing it felt to hear Matilda's voice again! How exhilarating it was to be leading the wolf! She let out a small laugh, as she jumped over a large tree root. Once and for all, she was going to rid herself of her child-hood fears...her greatest enemy. And, she would never let anyone else steal her childhood spirit, again. Not Damen, not Esmerelda, not the world.

As she darted through the trees towards the top of the bluff, the Forest Friends chased after Damen, trying to slow him down. The owls and birds flew in front of his face to distract him, while the squirrels hurled more acorns at his head. Even Penney's fox kits, who were growing bigger by the day, helped by nipping at Damen's tail.

Mittens clung to Fireball's antlers, as they raced after Damen. Matilda, even with her broken leg, was keeping pace with the rest of the Forest Friends, as if she still had four, strong legs.

"I've got to be almost there," Zoey said. Then, at last, she came to the edge of the tree line. She leaped as far as her legs could carry her, as she crashed through the last wall of the forest. Panting, and holding her head between her knees, she slowly looked up and gazed out over the still, peaceful countryside. She knew Damen would be here any second and was forever grateful that the Forest Friends had stalled him, even for a few moments.

As she looked out at the horizon, she brushed away her golden curls from her light blue eyes. Her usually perfect curls were now wild and tangled with sweat and dirt. Then, she heard the sound of breaking tree limbs.

"Damen!" she yelled, as she gritted her teeth and spun around to face her enemy.

She looked up to see Damen's still blood-red eyes staring at her.

Thump, thump, thump, thump!

She could feel the pounding in her chest. Somehow, she had managed to still hold on to the large tree branch, all this time. She didn't even remember carrying it after she had hit Damen with it. Gripping it like a baseball bat, her knuckles began to turn white.

"I'm going to enjoy this," said Damen, as he walked slowly towards her.

"So am I," said Zoey as she locked eyes with the wolf. She could hear his gruff voice now, but she wouldn't let it distract her.

Then he gave one last shake, to rid himself of the last two squirrels that were still clinging to his back.

Just then, Matilda jumped out of the thick trees, with Fireball not two steps behind her. "Damen, no!" she shouted.

And with this, Damen leaped on top of Zoey, knocking her to the ground. But, before he could take his first bite, Matilda gave him a swift kick. This caused him to tilt to the right, just long enough for Zoey to quickly crawl away and scramble to her feet. Before he could stand back up on his four paws, Zoey lifted the tree branch high above her head. Then, before she knew what had happened, Damen let out a fierce growl and gripped the tree branch tightly between his teeth.

Zoey, still gripping the tree branch with all her might, suddenly felt her stomach drop as she was lifted high up into the air. She weighed but a mere bag of feathers to him. Damen began to shake his head quickly, back and forth. And then, with an evil grin, he flung his head to the right and let go of the tree branch, causing Zoey to fall over the edge of the bluff.

"Nooo!!!" yelled Matilda. Matilda and Fireball barreled towards Damen, and, with the strongest kicks they could muster, sent the wolf tumbling over the edge of the bluff.

"Ahhhh!" he cried out, as his mangled gray fur went over the side of the bluff.

The Forest Friends all raced to look over the edge of the bluff. Below, they expected to find a lifeless Damen. But to their surprise, he was nowhere to be seen. The owls flew down to find him.

"Matilda...Fireball...I'm slipping!" cried out a familiar voice.

"Zoey!" they said, as they both looked at each other. As they peered over the edge of the bluff, they could see Zoey hanging on to the side of a protruding rock. Her legs dangled beneath her.

"Zoey, hang on!" cried out Matilda. She could see Zoey's fingertips starting to slip.

"I can't...I can't do this!" cried Zoey.

"Zoey, yes you can," said Matilda, in her gentle, motherly voice. "You beat Damen. You faced your fears...and you can hear us, again. You're strong enough to do this."

"I...I can't," cried Zoey.

"Zoey, listen to my voice. Swing your legs from side to side. We will grab you as you get closer. Don't you trust us?" Zoey looked up into Matilda's loving, gold eyes. Then, she saw all the Forest Friends peering over the edge with their big, round eyes.

"I can do this," Zoey said to herself. Then, with what little strength she had left in her arms, she tightened her grip on the rock and began to swing her legs back and forth, from side to side.

"Grab her!" yelled out Matilda, as Fireball grabbed her shoe between his teeth. The owls swooped down and clutched her shirt with their claws, as they flapped their wings. Then, the foxes grabbed on, too, and they all pulled back as hard as they could, lifting Zoey just high enough so that she could wrap her arms around Fireball's neck.

As they pulled her to safety, she crumbled on the ground, breathing heavily.

"Zoey, are you alright?" asked Matilda, as she nuzzled her gently with her head.

"Is he...is he gone?" asked Zoey.

"Yes, my dear," said Matilda. "He's gone."

Fireball nudged her with his head, to help her slowly stand up. As she brushed the dirt and sweat away from her eyes, she peered over the edge of the bluff.

"But...where did he...?" she asked, as her voice trailed off while looking over the bluff.

"Don't worry," said Mittens. "We will find him. He won't bother you or Rorey, ever again."

CHAPTER TWENTY-FIVE

Esmerelda Arrives

"What a beautiful night it is for a party!" said Esmerelda to herself, as she clasped her hands together while she walked up the sidewalk to the cottage. "By tonight, I will have Rorey's heart and childhood spirit, and I will rule this forest for eternity!" she laughed to herself. As she laughed, a swirling cold wind blew through the entire forest sending more brown leaves to the forest floor.

"Now, where is that measly mutt when I need him?" asked Esmerelda. She looked along the edge of the forest, her eyes scanning for the reflection of Damen's green eyes. "Oh, never mind him, I'll do this myself," she snapped.

As she walked towards the front porch of the cottage, her long white dress seemed to dance in the twilight. With her crooked half-smile, she took out her wand and poof! A bouquet of rainbow-colored wildflowers appeared. As she looked down at them, she plucked out one of the delicate petals and threw it on the ground.

"A simple peace offering to win the trust of that little brat's mother," she said under her breath. "Without winning over her mother, I will never get that little girl away from them, long enough to steal her heart."

As she started to ring the doorbell, Esmerelda could hear the sounds of talking and laughter coming from the backyard. She slowly walked around the side of the cottage, her eyes hungrily looking for the little girl with the dark curls. Then, she stopped in her tracks. Esmerelda could hear the *thump, thump, thump* of Rorey's racing heart.

Hearing and feeling the warmth of Rorey's heartbeat caused Esmerelda's knees to get weak. She ducked into a shadow and leaned up against the side of the cottage. Her terrible powers were slipping away. It had been too many years since she had stolen the heart of a child, and she needed Rorey's childhood spirit to keep her icy heart beating. If she failed, she knew she would lose her powers and turn back into a wretched mortal. "I must steal her heart tonight," she said.

"Mommy!" said Rorey, as she raced toward her mother in the backyard. "Look at what Rocky got for me!" As Ryann stooped down to the ground towards her, Rorey held out a little toy dog in her hands. "See? It's Chihuahua Lola!"

Meanwhile, the real Chihuahua Lola gave a low growl and a high-pitched bark, from inside the cottage. She and the basset hounds were sulking, for having been banished to the cottage during tonight's party.

"Well, that was very nice of you, Rocky," said Ryann, as she patted Rocky on the head. He smiled at her and then ran back to stand by his parents, who were chatting with Nana and Papa.

"My Daddy mows grass," Rocky suddenly proclaimed to Papa. It was another one of his fun-filled facts he liked to share, from straight out of the blue.

"He does?" laughed Papa.

"Yes, and my Daddy likes rock music, too."

Heather laughed and said, "He likes to tell everyone that."

His father, Jeff, laughed and shook his head.

"Mom, can we have dessert now?" pleaded Rocky, as he batted his big, dark blue eyes.

"When do we ever have dessert before dinner?" asked Heather, with a smile.

"I think...how about...maybe tonight we do that," smiled Rocky.

"Nice try, Mister," said Jeff.

"Tag Rocky, you're it!" laughed Rorey, as she tagged him on the shoulder.

"Now, you're it!" said Rocky, as he tagged her back on the shoulder. As he chased after her, she let out a squeal. They raced around the yard, playing their favorite game of hide and seek around *The Peekaboo Tree.*

As the children played, the rest of the neighbors began to arrive, including Yia Yia and Pop-Pop, who lived in another ranch, just down the way from the cottage. The children of the forest loved to play at Yia Yia and Pop-Pop's house, for there were always treats to eat, and crafts to make.

Laughter and music could be heard echoing off the trees, throughout the forest. Little did they all know, the danger that was lurking in their very midst. If they had known what evil awaited them, every child would be tucked away safely at home.

"Oh Esmerelda, you made it!" said Nana.

Every head turned to see the enchanting woman walking towards them in her dazzling white dress, carrying a bouquet of wildflowers.

"Well, of course, I did," said Esmerelda, in her sugary-sweet voice. "I wouldn't miss this for the world."

CHAPTER TWENTY-SIX

Zoey's Heart

A s Zoey tried to catch her breath, she glided her golden curls up and out of her face.

"Zoey, do you think you can make it to the cottage?" asked Matilda.

Zoey nodded her head. She took a step forward but collapsed to her knees.

"Gasp!" cried out the Forest Friends.

"She's too weak!" said Nosey Rosey. "Oh, what will we do now?"

"Yes, how can we stop Esmerelda now?" asked Zoro.

"I know!" yelled out Mittens. "Fireball, let's put Zoey on your back! All we need to do is get her there, and she can explain the rest!"

"Yes, that's a great idea!" concurred the Forest Friends to one another.

"Ok kid, we're going to go for a little ride," said Fireball, as he stooped his body down to Zoey. She wrapped her arms around his neck and slowly pulled herself up onto him.

"Don't run too fast, or she'll fall off," said Matilda.

Fireball nodded his head at his mother and let her lead the way. Matilda leaped through the trees back into the forest. She followed the main Deer Trail, as all of the Forest Friends marched along, behind her and Fireball.

The sun was almost set, and the full moon began to take over as the forest's nightlight. As Matilda trotted along the trail, Harry glided down from the sky, landing softly in front of her. Using his beak, he pulled a tree bark message from his bag.

Matilda, Esmerelda has arrived at the cottage.

"Thank you, Harry," said Matilda. "It won't be long now. We will save Rorey, tonight." Matilda turned to look at the Forest Friends. "The truth of Esmerelda's evil intentions will be shown, tonight."

The Forest Friends nodded almost in unison and continued to trot down the main Deer Trail, which led them through Deer Valley and then, at last, up the final steep hill to the cottage.

"Wait, stop!" cried out Zoey, suddenly.

"What is it, Zoey?" asked Matilda. "Are you hurt?"

Zoey shook her head fiercely, back and forth, and squinted her eyes shut. Then, she swung her leg over Fireball and hopped down, dropping her pink backpack to the forest floor.

"Matilda...what if...what if no one believes me?" asked Zoey.

Matilda stared at her with a loving gaze.

"I mean, this is crazy!" shouted Zoey, as she raised her hands in the air and then, clasped her hands over her eyes. "I'm supposed to be in college. But noooo...instead, I show up to the cottage unannounced, at NIGHT, covered in dirt, and tell them that I can hear animals and that there is a wicked witch! They are going to commit me, tonight!" she said. "Ugh, how can I be so reckless? Why did I have to follow you? What am I even doing here?" As she took her hands off her eyes, all of the Forest Friends stared at her with their loving, always understanding eyes.

"Zoey, this is who you are," said Matilda. "You're special. Never be afraid of being special."

"She's right, Zoey," said Mittens, as he hopped off of Fireball's head. "If the rest of the world had a childhood spirit like you, they would be so much happier."

Zoey let out a laugh. "Happier if they were like me? I have scratches on my cheeks and dirt in my hair. And, I'm talking to animals," laughed Zoey.

"Zoey, you never really lost the childhood spirit in your heart. So many others have. Somewhere along the way, they lost their imagination. Their spark. Their excitement over the little things in this world," said Matilda. "But you can help them get it back."

"That's right! Like seeing the winter's first snow," said Nosey Rosey.

"Or, running barefoot through the summer grass!" said Penney, while her kits yipped excitedly in agreement.

"Or, like stuffing your mouth full of acorns!" Mittens muffled, as he gathered up a bunch and shoved them into his mouth.

"Mittens, do you have to do that, right now?" grumbled Franklin.

This caused Zoey to laugh...and laugh...and laugh.

"Oh, I don't know what I would do without you all," said Zoey. "Thank you for showing me who I really am...and, for letting me know that it's ok."

"OK? It's better than OK. It's fantastic!" yelled Mittens, as he pumped his white paws into the air. "Now, let's go save Rorey!" he yelled, as he raced up Zoey's leg, then arm and then perched himself on her shoulder.

"Yes," laughed Zoey. "Let's go save my cousin. Let's go save Matilda's Forest."

CHAPTER TWENTY-SEVEN

The Witch's Spell

The party was fully underway, and Papa was so proud of the bonfire that he built. Nana was passing out sticks, so their guests could roast their marshmallows. As Esmerelda mingled, she couldn't help but keep a close eye on the little girl with dark curls. She could hear her heartbeat, as she raced around the yard laughing with delight, along with Rocky.

Then, she spotted the girl's mother. She smiled at guests as they passed by her. All seemed to be enchanted by her...all but Ryann, that is.

"A peace offering my dear," she said, as she smiled and held out the bouquet of wildflowers that she had been saving for Ryann.

Ryann raised an eyebrow and said, "Oh...thank you," rather curtly. Then, she turned her head and continued to talk to Nana.

"I really must sincerely apologize, once again," said Esmerelda.

Ryann turned around. "Mom, would you excuse us for a minute?" she said.

"Oh yes, of course. I see your father is handing out too many marshmallows to the kids, so I'll be right back," said Nana.

"You know, we don't know each other very well," said Ryann.

"Yes, yes, of course, but I'd love for that to change," said Esmerelda.

"That's exactly my point," said Ryann. "You and I are strangers, and my daughter is my entire world. So, you must understand why I took such an offense to you trying to take her somewhere, without so much as asking her mother first."

"Yes, yes, of course," said Esmerelda. In her head, she was seething at the thought of stooping so low, to apologize and grovel to a mere mortal. But, she knew she needed to gain her trust, to get to Rorey.

"I was just so excited to have new neighbors, and your daughter is so charming. I've never had any children of my own, but I do adore them!" said Esmerelda. "It gets rather lonely, for a widowed woman like me, all alone in this forest," she said with a lie, as she cast her eyes to the ground.

"All I have to keep me company these days is my dog," said Esmerelda, with a small laugh. "I'm afraid to live alone, but I feel better having him to protect me."

At hearing this, Ryann's heart began to melt a bit for Esmerelda.

"I didn't know you were a widow," she said. "I'm sorry to hear that. You're so young."

"Oh, it happened a couple of years ago," said Esmerelda. Lying always came so quickly and easily to her. "You'll forgive me if I come on a little bit too strong?" she asked.

Ryann gave her a warm smile. "Thank you again, for the flowers," she said. "I guess it would be alright if we became more acquainted with each other. We are going to be neighbors after all."

"Marvelous," said Esmerelda, as she clasped her hands together. "I'd love to make it up to you, and I have a grand idea! Why don't I share it with little Rorey and see what she thinks, first? After all, she knows her Mommy best!"

"Alright," said Ryann, with a smile.

"Rorey, darling, come here for a moment," called out Esmerelda.

Rorey stopped running and turned towards Esmerelda. She stopped and stared at her. Something about Esmerelda always made her hesitate.

"Come here, Rorey," said Ryann, as she waved to her.

Rorey smiled at her Mommy and began to run towards her.

"Mommy, Mommy...me and Rocky roasted marshmallows, and Papa said he would teach us how to catch fire fries!"

Ryann began to laugh. "I think you mean fire*flies*," she said.

"No, I meant fire fries," said Papa, with a wink.

"Stop it," said Nana, as she playfully slapped his arm. "You're always confusing the kids."

"Rorey, Esmerelda was going to ask you a question," said Ryann.

Esmerelda smiled at the child.

Thump, thump, thump!

She could hear Rorey's heartbeat so loudly now, that it made her feel faint. She quickly stooped to the ground and placed her hands on the forest floor. She motioned for Rorey to come closer. The wind began to howl, leaves swirled about the forest, and a chilling wind cut through the mild air.

"What was that?" asked Nana. "I hope it's not a storm coming in."

"No, it can't be," said Papa. I checked the weather earlier, and it's not supposed to rain for days.

Esmerelda leaned closer to Rorey, to whisper a secret in her ear.

"Stop!" a loud voice cried out, over the music. All eyes turned towards the voice.

"Esmerelda, get away from her!" shouted Zoey, as she stood with her hands at her sides. They were clenched into fists.

"Why that worthless mutt," said Esmerelda, under her breath. Can't even handle one small girl."

"Zoey!" cried out Nana. She and Papa hurried across the yard towards her. "Sweetheart, what on earth are you doing here?" asked Nana. "Oh dear, and what happened to you? You're covered in dirt, and your cheek is bleeding!" she said. "Let's get you inside so you can get cleaned up."

"I'm sorry," said Zoey. "I don't want to interrupt your party, but..."

"Interrupt us? Why that's nonsense!" said Papa. "You're always welcome here. After all, this is more your home than it has been ours."

"Yes, and you are family," said Nana. "So, tell us what is going on."

Zoey glared at the witch. She felt strong and powerful until she locked eyes with Esmerelda. Then, in an instant, all of her self-doubt and childhood fears came racing back. Esmerelda's stare made her feel five years old again.

"Zoey, would you like to pick wildflowers with me?" she could hear Esmerelda's voice say, in her head.

"She...she um..." mumbled Zoey, as she kept her eyes on Esmerelda. "She's trying to steal Rorey's heart," she suddenly blurted out.

"Steal her heart?" asked Nana, Papa, and Ryann at the same time.

"Yes. I know I sound crazy, but she tried to do the same thing to me when I was a little girl," said Zoey.

"Is everything ok?" asked Heather, as she came walking over. "Jeff was wondering if he could play his guitar around the campfire, now."

"What?" asked Papa. He shook his head and turned to look at Heather. "Oh...oh yes, of course, I'll turn down the music so he can play," said Papa. He looked back at Zoey, took a couple of steps backward, and turned to walk towards the speakers.

"I know this is really strange," said Zoey, as she looked towards the ground and kicked a pebble with her sneaker. "But, I just know Esmerelda is going to hurt Rorey," she said. "Matilda knows, too."

"Matilda?" asked Nana. "Now, who is Matilda?"

"She's the um...deer who lives here," said Zoey. "She helped save me from Esmerelda and the wolf when I was about Rorey's age. You can ask her, or any of the Forest Friends!"

"Oh, my," said Nana, as she covered her hand over her mouth. "Honey, why don't we go inside and talk some more about this," said Nana. She put her arm around Zoey's shoulder and started to guide her towards the house. "I'm sure moving away from home and going to university, has been very strange and new for you," said Nana gently. "We need to call your mother."

"I'm not crazy!" shouted Zoey, as she stomped her foot on the ground. "I know you don't want to believe me, but right now we have to protect Rorey!"

"Esmerelda, I'm sorry about all of this," said Nana, in a quiet voice. "I'm sure she's just dehydrated, and you can see that she's not well, right now," said Nana.

"Oh yes, the poor dear," said Esmerelda, as she shook her head.

"No, no, let go of me!" yelled Zoey, as Nana tried to take her by the hand.

Ryann took Rorey by the hand. "I think it's best if we go inside, now," said Ryann. "It is getting past her bedtime, anyway."

"No!" cried out Esmerelda, in a panicked voice. She put her hand on Ryann's shoulder, to stop her from walking away.

"What?" asked Ryann, in a confused voice.

"I...I mean...I didn't get a chance to tell Rorey about my idea for you, yet," said Esmerelda. Her vision began to blur, and the forest's trees appeared to be swaying back and forth in the distance. She knew she had to act fast before she lost her powers.

"Um, that's ok," said Ryann. "We can talk another time. Goodnight, then." Ryann turned and began to walk briskly into the house.

"Why, you little ingrate!" gritted Esmerelda through her teeth, as she glared at Zoey. "Twelve years ago, you may have gotten away from me. But, you're not going to stop me, tonight!" she shouted. "I had to suffer, as I waited for another child with a heart as strong as yours. Well, the time has come, and I want hers!" she shouted, as she pointed at Rorey.

Suddenly, the music died down and everyone at the party turned to look at Esmerelda. They muttered to themselves quietly, with a mix of confusion and terror on their faces.

"You're all such fools!" she said, as she began to laugh. Then, her dazzling white dress began to transform into blood red. The color seemed to spill from the top down to the bottom.

Then, a cold winter air blasted its way through the forest, sending every last leaf raining down, covering everyone who stood in its path, up to their knees.

As they looked down in disbelief, the leaves began to turn into fresh, white snow. Then, with her wand, Esmerelda sent a swirling cloud of red smoke around Rorey, who was now clutched in her mother's arms. Rorey's dad, Ricky, began to run towards them, but he was too late. Esmerelda pointed her wand at Rorey and lifted her out of her mother's arms. She began to float towards Esmerelda, as the Forest Friends began to charge towards the witch.

"Ahhhh!" screamed all of the guests, as they began to run in different directions, for fear of their lives.

"No!" cried out Rocky, as he ran towards Esmerelda and kicked her leg. She whirled around to face him, with her eyes flashing blood red.

"Rocky, my dear boy," said Esmerelda. "I think I will save your heart, for later!" She turned and pointed her wand at the boy. This caused Rorey to fall towards the ground.

Zoey dove to catch Rorey, just before she hit the forest floor.

"I tried to get you once, too, my boy," said Esmerelda. "But you were too smart for me, weren't you? Well, tonight you made the biggest mistake of your little life!"

As she lifted her wand high in the air, Matilda jumped through the crowd and gave her the strongest kick she could with her back legs. This sent Esmerelda crashing to the ground.

"Hahahaha.....Ahhahahaha!" bellowed Esmerelda. "Everyone, I'd like you all to meet my DEER sister, Matilda!"

Rocky got away from the witch and ran back to his parents, while Esmerelda was distracted. Heather and Jeff wrapped their arms tightly around him.

"You see, she was always so graceful. So loooving. So perfect," snapped Esmerelda. "Mommy and Daddy didn't even know that I was there. That is until she and her equally beloved son went missing. Oh, it was quite the tragedy, indeed," she laughed, as she stared at Matilda.

"The real tragedy is you, Esmerelda," said Matilda.

"Can anyone other than Zoey, even hear you?" laughed Esmerelda. "Oh Matilda, I really did make you invisible to this world, didn't I? Here you are talking away, and no one can hear you!" laughed Esmerelda.

"I can," said Rorey in a soft voice.

"You can what, Rorey?" asked Zoey, as she held her tightly.

"I can hear Matilda," she said.

"You can?" asked Zoey. "So, you can hear her, too?" she said.

"Yes, and I can hear Sniffles too," said Rorey.

"Sniffles...who's Sniffles?" asked Zoey, as she looked back at the Forest Friends.

"Yo...right over here," said Mittens, as he pointed to himself with his white mitten paws.

"Oh, I see!" said Zoey. "It must be because of your allergies, Mittens!" laughed Zoey.

"I don't know if I've had too much to drink tonight, or not enough," said Nana, as she put her hand on her forehead.

"Bark, bark, bark!" Chihuahua Lola and the basset hounds' hair were standing on end, as they looked out the large, sliding glass door that led to the patio.

As everyone turned to look at the barking dogs, Esmerelda used this to her advantage. She spun around, pointed her wand at Matilda, and with the flick of her wrist, turned her into a frozen statue.

"Noooo!" screamed out Zoey. She dove on top of Esmerelda, as Ryann took Rorey back in her arms and dashed towards the cottage.

"No, no, I must get her heart, tonight!" yelled out Esmerelda.

Zoey had pinned the witch down on her stomach, and she struggled as she tried to point her wand at Ryann, who was running away with Rorey.

"Say goodbye, little girl," said Esmerelda, through her gritted teeth, but not before Fireball came over to stomp out her wand.

"No...you little brat, Jax! Now, look what you've done!" she cried out. The witch began to become weaker and weaker, as Zoey began to feel a surge of strength.

"Now, you will never steal another childhood spirit again, you witch!" said Zoey.

The moment the witch's wand broke, a miraculous thing happened. The ice began to melt off of Matilda, and the snow around their knees began to turn into water, then to leaves, then back to green grass. All of the leaves returned to the trees, and the cold wind turned back into a mild breeze. The crickets, who had grown quiet, began their nightly concert songs, once again.

The witch, too weak to move or speak, watched in horror as her blood-red dress transformed back into her old clothing. She recognized it all too well—it was the last dress she had worn as a mortal before she became a terrible witch.

As the ice melted off of Matilda, Zoey raced to her friend and threw her arms around her neck, as she had always done.

"Matilda, we did it," said Zoey. "We got rid of the witch and the wolf."

Matilda shook the last bit of the water off of her. Then, she smiled at Zoey.

"Zoey, you did this, not me," she said.

Zoey looked at her, puzzled.

"Don't you see?" asked Matilda. "You conquered your child-hood fears. This wasn't about Esmerelda or the wolf, at all. It was about you, and knowing who you are."

Just then, a white glow surrounded Fireball. It swirled about him until no one could see him, anymore. When it was gone, a young boy with sandy brown hair was left in his place. Esmerelda's spell had been broken.

Matilda's eyes filled with tears as she looked at her son, Jax, for the first time in thirteen years.

Then, she turned to look back at Zoey.

"Zoey, I'm afraid I need to say goodbye, now," said Matilda.

"Goodbye? What...what do you mean?" asked Zoey, not fully comprehending what was about to happen.

Matilda nodded and smiled towards the young boy, who sat completely puzzled on the forest floor, with his hands on his head. Then, the same white glow appeared and swirled around Matilda. Zoey's big, blue eyes widened.

When it disappeared, a beautiful young woman with golden-brown hair stood in her friend's place. She wore a yellow sun-dress. Zoey couldn't believe what she saw, and Nana and Papa let out a loud gasp.

"Matilda?" asked Zoey. She walked closer to her and looked at her gold eyes. She recognized them right away and knew it was her dearest friend in the world.

CHAPTER TWENTY-EIGHT

The Young Woman

"Mommy, look!" said Rorey, as she pointed at the young woman.

The young woman looked at her hands, ran her fingers through her hair, and looked over at her young son.

"Mommy!" yelled Jax, as he ran towards her.

"My love!" Matilda said as she wrapped her arms tightly around him.

"Oh...Oh, I think I'm going to faint!" said Nana, as she began to sway back and forth. Papa caught her by the arm, just before she hit the ground.

"Mom, get a hold of yourself!" said Ryann, as she still clutched Rorey to her. She was standing close to the cottage's back door, still terrified of Esmerelda, and what she may try to do to Rorey.

Matilda, now a beautiful young woman, smiled at Zoey over her son's shoulder. She patted him on the back and said, "Everything's going to be alright, from now on."

He wiped the tears from his eyes and turned to hug Zoey who stood completely still with her arms at her sides. She didn't dare to blink for fear of what might happen in the split seconds that her eyes would be closed.

"Zoey, you look like you've seen a ghost," laughed Matilda.

"Your...your voice," stammered Zoey. "It's the same."

"Well, of course, it is," laughed Matilda. "You know, I haven't changed all that much. I'm still the same Matilda... except...wait!"

Matilda's eyes became big, as she looked down at her once broken right leg. She slowly took a step forward onto it. Then, realizing it was not broken, she began to run across the yard.

Meanwhile, Matilda's evil sister was still laying on the ground, with a circle of people and Forest Friends surrounding her. One of the party guests reached down and extended their hand, to help her off the ground.

"Get away from me, you vile mortals!" she griped, as she swatted them away with her hands. She refused to get up and instead sat on the ground, her dress covered in dirt.

Matilda turned around and dashed back to the crowd that had formed around Esmerelda. She stood and faced her sister. Esmerelda slowly looked up and locked eyes with her sister. The witch could feel the ice starting to melt around her heart.

"Well, you look lovely as always, sister," Esmerelda said, as her eyes began to fill with tears.

"I've waited all of my life to find the right words to say to you," said Matilda.

The two sisters stared at each other for a moment. Then, something rather unexpected happened. Matilda held out her hand. Esmerelda, her hand shaking, slowly reached to take it as Matilda pulled her up off the ground.

"Now, I've seen everything!" said Papa.

Nana turned to Zoey and took her by the hands. "I'm so sorry, I didn't believe you," she said, with tears in her eyes.

"I'm not sure I'd believe me, either," laughed Zoey.

"Mommy look, Sniffles!" said Rorey, as she pointed at Mittens. He was foraging through a bag of marshmallows that had been dropped on the ground in the chaos.

"Ahhh...Ahhh...Ahh...Chooo!" he sneezed.

"Oh Mittens, really!" griped Franklin.

Suddenly, all eyes were on Franklin.

"Did...did that possum just say something?" asked Heather.

Rorey and Zoey started giggling.

"I heard it, too!" said Ryann.

"So did I!" said Nana and Papa at the same time.

"You see, Zoey," said Matilda. "You really are special," she said, as she put her hand on her cheek.

"Come on, everyone!" yelled Papa. "Let's turn the music back up and welcome my niece, Zoey, back home!"

The crowd cheered, and everyone began to dance. Rorey and Rocky held hands with Zoey, as they danced around in a circle. Even the Forest Friends got in on the fun.

The sun had now set, and only the candles, the campfire, and the lightning bugs lit up the night sky.

As Zoey danced and twirled, she caught a glimpse of something green and glowing from deep within the forest's walls... something that looked like eyes. Or was it just the lightning bugs?

The End

**Did you enjoy
*Zoey and the Forest Friends?***

Consider leaving a review on Amazon to help
share this story with others!

**Want to see the real Matilda?
Visit emkellybooks.com**

**Zoey and The Forest Friends want to help
you find your childhood spirit.**
Use this page to write down something you haven't done
since you were a child. Now, go out there and do it!

We'd love to see your picture or video
of your childhood spirit! You can tag
#zoeyandtheforestfriends on Facebook and Instagram.

About the Author

E.M. Kelly (Erin Koch) is an award-winning writer, speaker, and advocate for children's wellness programs. As a certified fitness instructor and Generation Pound® Pro, she helps children build healthy bodies and self-esteem. She also served as a volunteer for Arise & Ski, which provides lessons to individuals with disabilities. She has earned numerous writing and marketing awards, including the 2018 Gold Quill Award of Merit for *Lifestyle* magazine, where she served as editor-in-chief. She lives in Troy, Missouri with her husband, Tommy, on 20 wooded acres. It was these woods, the forest's friendly animals, and the childhood spirits of her nieces and nephew, that inspired her to write her first book, *Zoey and the Forest Friends*.

CPSIA information can be obtained
at www.ICGtesting.com
Printed in the USA
LVHW040844191020
669132LV00003B/251